Mary Elizabeth Braddon

Gerard

The World, the Flesh, and the Devil. Vol. 3

Mary Elizabeth Braddon

Gerard
The World, the Flesh, and the Devil. Vol. 3

ISBN/EAN: 9783337049867

Printed in Europe, USA, Canada, Australia, Japan

Cover: Foto ©Andreas Hilbeck / pixelio.de

More available books at **www.hansebooks.com**

GERARD

THE WORLD, THE FLESH, AND THE DEVIL

A Novel

BY THE AUTHOR OF

"LADY AUDLEY'S SECRET," "VIXEN," "ISHMAEL,"
"THE DAY WILL COME"

ETC.

IN THREE VOLUMES

VOL. III.

LONDON

SIMPKIN, MARSHALL, HAMILTON, KENT & CO.
LIMITED

STATIONERS' HALL COURT

1891

LONDON:

PRINTED BY WILLIAM CLOWES AND SONS, LIMITED,

STAMFORD STREET AND CHARING CROSS.

CONTENTS OF VOL. III.

GERARD;

OR,

THE WORLD, THE FLESH, AND THE DEVIL.

CHAPTER I.

"HOW COULD IT END IN ANY OTHER WAY?"

THE winter was mild, one of those moist and gentle seasons which delight the heart of the sportsman, but which all the sanitarians and ultra sensible people declare to be unhealthy, preaching their little sermon about want of aëration, and so on. Gerard was not one of these. He hated frost and snow, London snow most of all; and he was glad of a winter which did not oblige him to leave Hester for any length of time. He did not want to spend all his days at the Rosary. She had made that once delightful retreat in some-wise a horror to him; but he loved her still, and

he shrank from any act that might seem like
desertion. When the year of Mrs. Champion's
widowhood was over he would have to face his
difficulty, and settle with himself and with his
first and second love as to what his life was to be.
By that time Nicholas Davenport might be
peacefully at rest, and the chief impediment to
his marriage with Hester removed. In the meantime Hester was to him in all things as dear and
as honoured as if she had been bound to him
by the strongest tie the law can forge—not a
very strong tie it must be admitted nowadays.
He stayed in town for about ten days, choosing
his sister's wedding present, and seeing all the
town had to show him in the way of dramatic
talent. He gave a couple of his famous breakfasts
during those ten days, and Hillersdon House was
put in working order, his staff of servants revised
and corrected, and every detail of his luxurious
surroundings carefully supervised. Valet and
butler were told that their master would winter
in England, mostly in London. Valet and butler
were fully aware that their master had another
establishment; but he had so far been cleverer
than the average master in keeping the secret

of the second home. No one knew where he went when he left Hillersdon House. He who was so amply furnished with carriages always went to the station in a hansom.

He spent Christmas at the Rosary, three days of quietness and contentment, which were a relief after the breakfasts, the copious talk, the picture galleries and theatres, the scandals, and perpetual movement of London. He would have been quite happy but for the uncomfortable consciousness of Nicholas Davenport's presence in the room above—an existence which he could never contemplate without vague pangs of remorse, lest this death in life were indeed his work, lest it had been that blow of his which shattered the feeble intellect. Hester told him what Mr. Mivor had said about the inevitableness of the attack; but this one opinion was not enough for comfort. Another doctor and a better doctor might have told a different story.

Hester tried to be happy in those brief days of holiday; but the old unquestioning happiness, the joy that looked neither before nor after, was gone. The perfect union was broken. The ring which symbolises eternity was snapped into mere

segments of life which she must accept with
thankfulness. It was much that her lover had
not deserted her. All the stories that she had
ever read went to prove that desertion was the
inevitable end of forbidden bliss such as she had
tasted. He had shown her that he could live
happily for more than a week apart from her,
but there was yet no hint of desertion; and he
had done much in deferring his journey to
Devonshire till after Christmas.

He left her on a mild and sunny morning,
looking far better than on his arrival at the
cottage. Those few quiet days had rested him
after the high living and keen contest of malicious
wit which constituted London society, or that
section of it in which he moved.

Hester and he had walked in the wintry woods
together, and enjoyed the balmy air of pine
thickets, and the soft carpet of fallen leaves,
with all the winter charm of chastened colouring
under grey skies. He told her at parting that
he had been very happy.

"If you could only have given me a little
more of your time it would have been better,"
he said. "You are so severe in your recognition

of a divided duty. Forgive me, love," he added hastily, seeing her look of distress. "You are all goodness, and I am a wretch to murmur. I will write to you after the wedding."

"Oh, sooner than that, Gerard; that would mean quite a week to wait!"

"Well, then, sooner. But you know what a bad correspondent I am. I think volumes about her I love, but my lazy pen refuses to write a single page."

He was gone, and she went back to the cottage, which had taken a different look since the change in its master's habits. It no longer looked like Gerard's home. It had the air of a house to which a man comes occasionally, and where things hardly bear the stamp of his individuality. The despatch-box was shut; the writing-table showed no litter of scattered papers. The books he read oftenest—Swinburne, Baudelaire, Richepin, Verlaine, Comte, Hartmann, Darwin, Schopenhauer, were all in their places; for these were books which Hester loved not, and she had not disturbed them in his absence. The rooms looked to her like the rooms in a widow's house. There was the absence of litter which marks the absence of man.

She sat by the fire in the study for an hour or more while the invalid was being dressed and got ready for his morning airing, sat thinking of her own life and what she had made of it; a melancholy review, for her conversation with Mr. Gilstone had swept away all sophistry as to her position. She no longer compared herself to Shelley's Mary, no longer believed in the rightfulness of her conduct. She stood convicted in her own eyes as a woman who had sinned. Whether the universe were or were not directed by a thinking mind, she had lost her place among good women. She sat there alone at this Christmas season, when other women were surrounded by friends, and told herself that she had forfeited the right to womanly friendship.

She walked beside her father's chair in the lanes for an hour before the brief winter day began to fade, walked at his side, and talked to him, and pointed out the features of interest in the landscape, the moving life of beast and bird, as she would have done for a child. She listened to his feeble, disconnected talk. She made him understand—as much as it was in his power to understand anything—that he was cherished and cared for.

They did not meet many people in the lanes, but those whom they met took a great deal more notice of the old man in the bath chair and the pensive face and girlish figure of his companion than Hester supposed.   Gentle and simple were interested—the simple with an unalloyed friendliness towards helpless old age and filial duty; the gentle with a touch of pity for the old man, mixed with conflicting opinions about his daughter.

The Curate in his soft felt hat, slouched over his brows as if he had been a brigand, the Misses Glendower, bent on district visiting, Mrs. Donovan driving her self-willed ponies, and crimson with the effort of keeping them under control—all these were keenly observant of Hester, and talked of her with a new zest at afternoon-tea.

This appearance of an invalid father, who, although physically and mentally a wreck, looked like a gentleman, was calculated to modify the village idea of Mrs. Hanley's position.   That she should have her father to live with her, clad in purple and fine linen, sedulously waited upon, and enthroned in a bath chair that must have cost as much as the family landau which Lady Isabel had just obtained from the Repository in Baker Street, certainly supplied an element of respectability which the world of Lowcombe had not looked for from Mrs. Hanley. After all, people are not kites, and though they may tear and maul a reputation they are not altogether without tenderness for the sorrows of life.

"I must say that young woman's attention to her father is one of the most touching things I have seen for a long time," said Mrs. Donovan, "and if I could have stopped my ponies yesterday morning I really think I should have pulled up and introduced myself to her. But there, you all know what my ponies are."

"Yes, Mrs. Donovan, and we all know what your driving is," answered Lady Isabel, who had been a famous whip in her youth, and who, belonging to a house that had always been poor, liked to show her contempt for the newly rich.

"I really think some of us ought to call," pursued Mrs. Donovan, ignoring the venomed shaft. " I hear that Mr. Hanley has been a good deal away from home lately." .

" Has he ? The beginning of the end, I should think. Why don't you call, Mrs. Donovan? You are broader-minded than I am, and you have no daughters. It can't do you any harm to take notice of Mrs. Hanley; and as she doesn't know a soul in the place she may be glad to make your acquaintance."

" I don't think she could do your daughters any harm, Lady Isabel. She is so much younger than your girls; and she looks the picture of innocence."

" Yes, and I have seen just such pictures in the Burlington Arcade, when I have been to my glover's rather too late in the afternoon," retorted Lady Isabel. " You can please yourself, Mrs. Donovan ; but I never visit people whose ante-cedents I don't know. The fact that this young person behaves nicely to her imbecile father is no evidence of her respectability. Young persons of that class have their feelings as well as we have, and I dare say they are fonder of their own people than we are, knowing themselves shut out of society."

After this Mrs. Donovan gave up all idea of patronising Mrs. Hanley. However she might hug herself with the thought of her investments and dividends, and the power which unlimited cash can give, she knew that she was not strong enough to fly in the face of Lowcombe society. It was for her to follow, and not to lead, if she wanted to be admitted to that inner circle, where the society was not suburban and rich, but county and arrogantly poor. These county people boasted of their dearth in these latter days, as if it were a distinction; since poverty, for the most part, meant land, while wealth not unfrequently meant trade. Mrs. Donovan wanted to stand well with that choice circle which had its ramifications in the Peerage, and talked of Dukes and Duchesses as if they were men and women: so she did not call upon Mrs. Hanley; and thus Hester was spared that favour which would have been the last worst drop in her cup of bitterness.

New Year's Eve is apt to be a saddening season, even in the family circle, for however cheerily we may pretend to take it with carpet dances and

hand-shaking, or Pickwickian jovialities in the
way of innocent games and strong drinks, there
lurks deep in every heart the consciousness of
another stage passed in the journey that leads
down hill to that inn we all wot of, where there
is always room for everybody : and deep in every
heart there is the memory of some one whom the
year has taken away, and not all Time's years
can bring back. But what of New Year's Eve to
the lonely girl who sat beside the fire through the
long evening, surrounded with the books she
loved, but finding scanty solace even in their
company !

Such lonely evenings are by no means rare in
the lives of wedded wives, at those seasons when
the indisputable rights of gun or rod keep the
sportsman far away from the home fireside, or
when the sacred demands of business constrain
the mercantile man to over-eat himself in a city
hall : but Hester could not forget that she was
sitting alone to listen for the ringing of the midnight joy-bells, only because she was an unwedded
wife. Had the bond been sanctified her natural
place would have been with her husband at
Helmsleigh Rectory on this vigil, which was a

memorable one for the Rector's household, since
it was the eve of his only daughter's wedding.
How natural that she, Lilian's friend, should
have been by Lilian's side to-night. How indispensable her presence had she been Lilian's
sister-in-law. Tears sprang to her aching eyelids
at the humiliating thought that she could now
be no more counted worthy to enter that home
where she had once been treated almost as a
daughter of the house.

She remembered a New Year's Eve spent in
that house, ever so many years ago, as it seemed
to-night, looking back from a life in which all
things were changed, across a dreary interval of
misfortune and poverty. She remembered how
kind every one had been to her, full of tenderest
compassion for her motherless youth, her burden
of household cares. How bright and happy the
rambling old Rectory had looked, all the sitting-
rooms gaily lighted with a miscellaneous collection
of lamps and candles ; the old-fashioned Christmas
decorations of holly and evergreen in hall and
dining-room ; the friendly evening party, with a
good deal of music and a little waltzing, started
in an impromptu fashion by the youthful master

of the neighbouring hounds; the inevitable recitation from the curate of an adjoining parish —long, dismal, intended to make people's flesh creep, but only making the aged yawn and the young laugh. She and Lilian had sat together in a corner by the piano, struggling against the tendency to girlish giggling, full of their own small jokes and depreciation of the youth of the neighbourhood, both of them heart-whole and happy—happy as children are, without thought of the morrow.

She had played, fresh from her German master's tuition, full of the Leipsic school and its traditions, had played and had been praised and made much of. Her playing was a thing of the past almost, for in the days of her poverty she had been without a piano, and in her new life she had given up'all her hours to being Gerard's companion, and he, who cared little for classical music, had given her no encouragement to regain lost ground by severe practice. The pretty little cottage-piano stood in its corner unopened, and now that it might have been to her as a companion and friend, she feared to play lest the sounds should disturb her father in his rooms on the upper floor.

The night was clear and frosty, but not severely cold, and at midnight she wrapped a thick shawl about her and went out on the lawn, and walked slowly up and down by the star-lit river, listening for the bells of Lowcombe Church. They broke out upon the stillness with a sudden burst of sound that thrilled her, like the spontaneous cry of some Titanic soul rejoicing in some great, nameless good to mankind. She could not divide herself from the gladness in that burst of music, as the sounds came pealing along the water. The starlight, the darkness of the opposite woods, the faint ripple of the quiet river, the universal hush of calmest winter night through which the joy-peal broke, were all too much for her sad, remorseful heart. She felt that somewhere beyond this narrow scene of life there must be a home and a refuge for lives such as hers, somewhere a friendship and a pity greater than human pity, which could understand, and pardon, and shelter. If it were not so the story that church bells, and running rivers, and winds that blow over woodland and mountain, and cathedral organs had been telling was a lying message to mankind, civilised and uncivilised, in all the ages that were gone; and that fond hope deep in the heart of man, barbarian or civilised, bond or free, was the cruellest hallucination that was ever engendered in that automatic instrument which we call mind.

She walked for nearly an hour in the wintry garden, and that quiet commune with Nature, that unconscious absorption of the beauty of the winter landscape gave her much more comfort than she had been able to find in Tennyson or Browning, since even "In Memoriam," which was to her as a second gospel, had failed to-night to wean her from the thought of her own sorrows.

"I wonder if he has remembered me, once, just for one moment, in all this evening," she asked herself, as she rose from her knees.

Even when most shaken in her old faith by the new learning she had never altogether lost the old habit of prayer. Her prayers might be vague and indistinct, the outpouring of a sorrowful mind, to what God she knew not, but for her prayer was a necessity of life.

She was sitting at her lonely breakfast next

morning in Gerard's study, when something happened which cheered her with the knowledge
that she was not altogether forgotten.

There came the sound of wheels on the crisp
gravel drive, a loud ring at the door, and then
the country-bred parlour-maid bounced into the
room with an excited air, exclaiming, "If you
please, ma'am, here's a brougham!"

"What do you mean, Pearson? It's the doctor,
I suppose!"

"No, no, ma'am. It's a new carriage, coachman, and all complete—for you! Here's a letter
the coachman brought. I forgot the salver, I
was that taken aback," and the damsel handed a
letter.

It was from Gerard.

"DEAREST,

"Since you are to spend the winter
in the country you must have a carriage, so I
send you a brougham by way of New Year's gift.
It has been built specially for country work, and
will be none the worse for much service in the
rustic lanes you are so fond of. The coachman
has admirable testimonials from previous em-

ployers, so you may trust him fully as head of your stable. I have told him to engage a stable-help, and to put all things on a proper footing. The horse was bought for me by a man who is a far better judge of the species than I am.

"Be happy, my love, in the beginning of the year, and in many a happy year to come.

"Your ever faithful, G. H.

"P.S.—Just starting for Devonshire."

The letter made her almost happy, almost, but not quite, for kind as his words were they gave her no assurance of his love; they did not tell her that his thoughts and his heart's desire would be with her at the beginning of the year, the first year which had begun since they two had loved each other. For him it was much less of an epoch than it was for her, and he had easily reconciled himself to the idea of their separation.

The gift vouched for his kindly thought of her, and was welcome on that account, but she felt that any addition to her luxuries only accentuated the dubiousness of her position.

She went out to look at the brougham, a delightful carriage, small, neat, with dark, subdued colouring, and a perfection of comfort and elegance which in no way appealed to the eye of the casual observer; such a brougham as a leading light of the House of Commons might choose to convey him quickly and quietly to and from the scene of his triumphs, every detail sober, simple, costly only because of its perfection. The horse was a fine up-standing brown, a patrician among horses, carrying his head as if he were proud of it, doing his work as if hardly conscious of doing it, in the fulness of his power; an amiable horse, too, for he stooped his lordly head and gave his velvet nose freely to the caressing touch of Hester's hand.

The coachman was middle-aged, and, to all appearance, the pink of respectability.

" I have only driven from the station, ma'am," he said. "If you'd like to drive this afternoon the horse won't hurt."

" No, no. I'll let him rest to-day, if you please."

" Quite the lady," thought the coachman, as he drove round to his unexplored stables, pleased with a mistress who showed no impatience to be sitting in her new carriage and running her new horse off his legs; evidently a lady to whom a brougham was no novelty.

He had been pleased with his master, who had told him to order whatever was required in the way of stable gear, and to engage a helper, all in the easy way which marks a master who does not look too closely into details.

Hester was comforted by this mark of Gerard's regard. For a millionaire to give such gifts might have but little significance, yet the gift implied thoughtfulness, and it made her happier to know that he had thought of her.

She drove in her new carriage on the following day, drove to Reading and made her little purchases, all as modestly chosen as if she had been the wife of a curate. Gerard had given her a pocket-book stuffed with bank-notes before he left for Devonshire, but no plethora of money could induce her to extravagant expenditure. Her winter gowns, made by a Reading tailor, were of a Quaker-like plainness; her dinner-gown of soft grey silk was the simplest thing in home dinner-gowns. The long seal-skin coat which Gerard had insisted upon ordering for her at the beginning of the winter was the only expensive garment she possessed. Just at this season she had to make purchases which were not for her own use, purchases of finest lawn and softest cambric, and pattern garments of daintiest form, which gave employment to her skilful fingers in the long lonely evenings of that first week in the New Year.

Gerard wrote to her of his sister's wedding in briefest phrases. Must he not also have remembered that had all been well she should have had her place, and an honoured place, at that family gathering, and that there must be a sting in anything he might write of the ceremony and of his people?

"They left for the Land's End, to spend a fortnight in a little inn on the edge of the Atlantic—a curious fancy for a winter honeymoon. I wanted them to go to Naples and Sorrento—of course at my expense—but John Cumberland would not hear of a journey that would keep him away from his parish for more than a fortnight, and my sister's mind is his mind, so they are clambering about upon the rocks, watching the shags and the gulls, and listening to the roaring of the breakers—utterly

happy, I believe, in each other's society, as you
and I have been beside the dripping fringes of
the willows. For my own part, I can hardly
imagine a January honeymoon. Love needs sunshine and long summer days."

That last sentence haunted Hester all through
the evening, as she bent over her work at her
little table in the nook by the fire. Was love
ended with a single summer? Could she and
Gerard ever renew the happiness of last summer?
Alas, no; for last summer he could hardly bear
to be absent from her for an hour; and of late he
had shown her only too plainly that he could
live without her. It was only natural, perhaps.
Who but a romantic girl could ever think that
any union love ever made could be one long
honeymoon? There was no word of returning
to the Rosary in Gerard's last letter. His mother
insisted on his staying for another week at the
Rectory, and he had been unable to refuse her.
He hoped that Hester was taking long drives,
getting herself plenty of new books at Miss
Langley's delightful library, and keeping in good
health and spirits. It is so easy for the absent
to entertain these hopes.

Hester did not take many drives, though the roads were in good condition, and the coachman came every morning for orders. She preferred her quiet walks beside her father's bath chair; for these at least left the satisfaction of duty done, and the brougham, with all its elegant luxuriousness, only oppressed her with a keener sense of her position. She felt ashamed of driving past the Lowcombe people in their shabbier carriages, felt almost as if she could hear the hard things they said of her.

She thought often of kindly Mr. Gilstone and his vain endeavour to set things right for her, and she longed for the sound of his friendly voice in her solitude. But she had no hope that he would ever enter the Rosary again. She would have gladly gone to his church on the first Sunday of her solitude, had she been brave enough to face the curious eyes of his congregation; but on the second Sunday she felt so utterly desolate that her heart yearned to the church as the one shelter outside her lonely home where she could enter and feel herself unforbidden, so in the evening she ordered her brougham and drove to Lowcombe, telling her coachman to stop at the entrance to the village, and to wait for her at the same spot when the service was over. She did not want to make herself conspicuous at the lych gate by the flaming lamps of her carriage, or the beauty of her horse. She hoped to creep quietly to a seat in one of the aisles; but it happened that the pew opener was the son of the butcher who served the Rosary, and was eager to pay all possible honour to a good customer. With this intent he conducted her to a seat near the pulpit, the seat of the august Mr. Muschatt himself, a seat cushioned and foot-stooled in purple cloth, where the local landowner sat like Dives, and was reported never to drop more than sixpence into the bag, and only to drop sixpence when he had failed in obtaining a threepenny piece. Here, in the sight of the evening congregation, which included most of the gentilities of Lowcombe, where the evening service was popular, Hester sat in her sealskin coat and neat little sealskin toque and heard the evening lessons, and here she knelt with meekly bent head and joined in the prayers which had once been interwoven with her daily life, but which now had a doubly impressive sound after a silence of half a year; while the old hymn tunes, and most of all, the words of that evening hymn she had loved so well—"Abide with me, fast falls the eventide," moved her almost to tears. Indeed it was only the consciousness of the lamplight on her face, and perhaps, too, the apprehension of furtive glances from unkind eyes, that nerved her to the effort which restrained her tears.

The Rector's evening sermon was simple and practical, one of those plain-speaking, homely addresses which he loved to give of an evening —sermons in which he spoke to his flock as to a little family with whose needs and sorrows and failings he was familiar. Hester met his glance more than once as she looked up at him, and there were words, comforting words, in his sermon which she fancied were meant especially for her, words to lighten the sinner's despair and to promise the dawn of hope.

She went home happier for that village service, and having once confronted the curious looks of the congregation she determined to go to church regularly. The church was open to sinners as well as saints, to Magdalen as well as to Martha and Mary, to the doubter as well as to the believer; and now that Gerard was no longer by to assail the creed in which she had been reared, with all the pessimist's latest arguments, her heart went back into the old paths, and the Rock of Ages was once again a shelter and a support.

There was a daily service at Lowcombe, and to this service Hester went every morning during Gerard's absence. It was the one break in her life, an hour of quiet prayer and contemplation which tranquillised her mind, and sustained her through the monotonous duties of the day.

Gerard reappeared after more than a fortnight's absence. His native air had not improved his health. He looked haggard and weary, and owned that he had been bored in the family circle.

"My father and mother are model people of their kind," he said, "and everything in their house goes by clockwork; but so does life in a gaol, and I confess that I found the Rectory about as lively as Portland. There was nothing to do, and nothing to think about. If I had been a sportsman I should have been out with the hounds. Rural life provides nothing for men who are not sportsmen. Such malshapen beings are hardly believed in by the rural mind."

Hester saw with poignant grief that after a few days at the Rosary Gerard was as bored as he had been in Devonshire. He did not hint at this weariness, but the signs of ennui were too obvious. He suggested inviting Justin Jermyn, but Hester had grown keenly sensitive of late, and she was so evidently distressed at the mention of Mr. Jermyn, that Gerard did not press the question.

"I feel as if there is a covert sneer in almost every word Mr. Jermyn speaks to me," she said.

"Indeed, my dear child, you wrong him. Jermyn is a laughing philosopher, and holds all things lightly. I envy him that lightness as the happiest gift Nature can bestow. For him, to exist means to be amused. He lives only for the present hour, has a happy knack of utilising his friends, and does not know the meaning of thought or sorrow."

Gerard went to London soon after this little discussion about Jermyn, and was away till the end of the week, and from thenceforward he appeared at the Rosary only for two or three days at a time, coming at shorter or longer intervals, his periods of absence lengthening as London began to fill. In London Jermyn was much with him, his umbra, his second self. Hester discovered this fact from his conversation, in which Jermyn's name continually recurred. He spoke of the man always with the same scornful lightness, as of a man for whom he had no real affection, but the man's society had become a necessity to him.

"Does he live upon me?" he said once, when Hester gently suggested that Mr. Jermyn must be something of a sponge, "well, yes, I suppose he does—upon me among other friends—upon me perhaps more than any other friend. You remember how Lord Bacon used to let servants and followers help themselves to his money, while he sat at his desk and wrote, seemingly unobservant. Bacon could not afford to do that kind of thing—his income wouldn't stand it—but Jermyn is my only follower, and I can afford to let him profit by my existence. He does not sponge or borrow my money. He only wins it. I am fond of piquet, and when we are alone he and I play every night. He is by far the better player, an exceptional player indeed, and I dare say his winnings are good enough to keep him in pocket money—while I hardly feel myself any poorer by what I lose. If you would spend a little more, Hettie, I should be all the better satisfied."

"You are only too generous," she said, with a sigh. "I have everything in the world that I want—and I have been more extravagant lately. Your bank notes seem to slip through my fingers."

"That is what they were meant for. I'll send you another parcel from London to-morrow."

"No, no, please do not. I have plenty of money, nearly three hundred pounds. But are you really going back to town to-morrow?"

"Really, dear. It is a case of necessity. My lungs won't stand this river-side atmosphere. Why don't you think better of my suggestion, Hester, and let me find another home for your father. He could be well provided for, and

you would be free to travel with me. Dr. South
would think me mad if I were to spend February
and March in the valley of the Thames—and
even you would hardly wish me to run so great
a risk."

"Even I. Oh, Gerard, as if your life were
more precious to any one in this world than
it is to me."

"Prove your regard for me, then. Let me
arrange at once about your father—there are
plenty of respectable households in which he
could be placed under medical care—and come
to Italy with me."

"No," she sighed, "that is what I should love
to do, but I have made up my mind. While
my father lives I will do my best to make
his life happy. It is the only atonement I can
make——"

Her tears finished the sentence. Gerard rose
impatiently, and began to walk about the room.

"You can hardly expect me to sacrifice my
life to your exaggerated ideas of duty," he
said. "The best part of the world is untrodden
ground for me, and I live in an age which has
minimised the fatigue and difficulty of travel-

ling. A man may go round the world now more easily than he went from London to Paris a hundred years ago, and I have means to make the uttermost expenditure a legitimate outlay. And you would have me wither under such a sky as that"—he pointed to the grey fog that veiled garden and river, and blotted out the opposite shore—"and restrict my movements to jogging backwards and forwards between London and this house."

"I would have you do nothing, Gerard, that you do not like, nothing that can possibly injure your health. If it is best for you to go to the South, go there without an hour's needless delay. I will try to make the best of life while you are away, and you will come back to me in the summer, won't you, Gerard, if you are not tired of me?"

"Tired of you. You know that I am not. Don't I entreat you to go with me? It is only your whims and exaggerated notions I am tired of."

This conversation occurred in February, and it may be that the dull, depressing February weather, the river fog, the Scotch mist, the sodden grass and dripping shrubs, and dark, leafless branches of beech and elm, counted for something in Gerard's angry impatience. He went back to London on the following day, and he talked of starting for Italy, nay, indeed, made all his plans for departure, and then at the last altered his mind, and stayed in town.

He reappeared at the Rosary at the end of the week, and it was a shock to him to find Nicholas Davenport installed by the drawing-room fire. There had been a gradual improvement in his condition since Christmas, and the doctor had suggested his being carried downstairs in his invalid chair of an afternoon, thinking that the change of surroundings might have a beneficial influence upon his mental state. His mind had certainly been brighter. He had taken more heed of Hester's presence, and had talked to her rationally, though without memory, frequently repeating the same speeches, and asking the same questions over and over again.

His presence beside the hearth made the house odious to Gerard, who saw in that bent and shrunken form the image of death. He retreated at once to the study, where Hester found him standing beside the fire in a gloomy reverie.

"I had no hope of your coming to-day," she said deprecatingly, "or I would not have had my father brought down to the drawing-room. I'm afraid it hurts you to see him there."

"It does, Hester. The very consciousness of his presence in the house has always been a horror to me. Perhaps it is because my own life hangs upon so thin a thread that I hate to see the image of death—and that living death of imbecility is death's worst form. Sometimes I think I shall die that way myself."

She soothed him, and argued away his fears about himself, and promised that her father's presence should not again be inflicted upon him, come when he might to the Rosary. She would remember her divided duty, and she would take care that the home which he had created should be made happy for him.

"It is your house," she said. "I ought to remember that."

"There is no yours nor mine, Hettie," he answered kindly. "All I possess of this world's

gear is at your service; but I am full of fancies,
and your father's presence chills my soul."

He had come to the Rosary on Saturday
afternoon, meaning to stay till Monday, and
then go back to London and reconsider his
migration to the South. He had been somewhat disheartened by being told at his club
that there was snow in Naples, and that people
were leaving Rome in disgust at the Arctic
cold. These evil rumours, together with his
yearning to see Hester once more, had delayed
his departure. He had been feeling very ill
all the week, and he told himself he must
lose no time in getting to a balmier climate,
wherever it was to be found.

He did not return to town on Monday. He
was shivering and depressed all through Sunday,
to Hester's extreme anxiety, and on Sunday
night he yielded to her entreaties, and allowed
her to send for Mr. Mivor, who found all the
symptoms of lung trouble. The trouble declared
itself before Monday night as acute inflammation
of the lungs, complicated by a feeble heart; and
for three weeks the patient hung between life
and death, tenderly and devotedly nursed by

Hester, who rested neither night nor day, and accepted only indispensable aid from the hospital nurse who had been sent for at the beginning of the attack. When Gerard was able to go down to the drawing-room as a convalescent, he was hardly whiter or more shadowy-looking than Hester herself. He was not ungrateful. He knew the devotion that had been given to him, knew that in those long nights of pain and semi-delirium one gentle face had always watched beside his bed; yet after the first few days of convalescence an eager desire for change of surroundings took possession of him. That illness, coming upon him suddenly, like the grip of demoniac claws fastening upon lungs and heart, had given him a terrible scare. He had been told that he had not a good life; but not since his childhood had he felt the paralysing power of acute disease. Never perhaps until now had he realised the frailty of the thread which held all he knew of or believed in—this little life and its pleasures. In his new terror he was feverishly eager to get to a better climate, to Italy, to Ceylon, to India, anywhere to escape the bitter treacheries of English weather.

Jermyn came down to see him, at his earnest desire. Jermyn played piquet with him in the long March evenings, and amused him with the news of the town; but even this did not lessen his horror of the house that held Nicholas Davenport, or his ever-present terror of a relapse. He arranged the details of his journey with Jermyn, who knew exactly what kind of weather they were having along the Western Riviera.

"You will find summer by the Mediterranean," he said ; "March and April are the most delicious months on that sunny shore. Nature is loveliest there just when all the smart people have left for Paris or London. Leave everything to me and your valet, and all you will have to do when your conscientious little medical man here permits you to move, will be to take your seat in the *train de luxe*. I am going Southward for Easter myself, and I'll be your travelling companion, if you like."

"If I like? I should be miserable alone. You will go as my guest, of course."

"As you please," replied Jermyn, shrugging his shoulders. "One does not stand upon punctilio with a millionaire on a matter of

pounds, shillings, and pence. I hope to earn
my travelling expenses by being useful to you.
Does Mrs. Hanley go with you to the South?"

"No," Gerard answered shortly.

Mr. Jermyn went up to town next day to see
Gerard's valet, and to give all instructions for the
journey. He came back in time for dinner.

"Mrs. Hanley shuns me," he said, on this
second occasion, he and Gerard having dined
alone on both evenings. "I hope I have not
offended her."

"She likes to be with her father."

"But surely some one told me that the old
gentleman goes to bed at eight o'clock. She
can hardly be wanted in his room after that
hour."

"Perhaps not, but she may like to be there,"
answered Gerard, and then changed the conversation abruptly. "How is your friend the painter
getting on with his house?"

"Admirably. I believe it will be finished in
two years, which is only a year and a quarter
beyond the time specified. His contract with
the builder was for two thousand five hundred,
and I fancy, in spite of all his alterations and

improvements on the original design, he will get off for six or seven thousand. He finds his boat too cold a residence at this time of year, and he is staying at the Inn, where he puts me up."

" I am sorry we have no room for you here——"

"Don't mention it. I doubt whether Mrs. Hanley would like to have me on the premises even were there half-a-dozen bachelor rooms. I'm afraid I am no favourite of hers. It is a curious thing that while the ladies I meet at the Petunia and the Small Hours are positively devoted to me I am unfortunate in provoking the prejudices of the purely domestic mind—and Mrs. Hanley is so thoroughly domestic."

"She is the most devoted and unselfish of women. Her only faults are virtues in excess," answered Gerard, gravely.

His convalescence lasted a week longer before the village doctor gave him leave to start for the Riviera, where the weather reports were now of the fairest. His illness had been so carefully watched by Mr. Mivor that he had implicit belief in that gentleman's wisdom, and listened without impatience to the counsel which the doctor gave him on his last visit, counsel which in some points echoed Dr. South's advice, given some months earlier.

Illness is apt to be selfish, and in his long illness that self-love which had grown and strengthened ever since the sudden change in his fortune, took a stronger growth, and in the long days of convalescence, weak, depressed, and self-absorbed, he had brooded over Hester's refusal to be his companion in his Southern wanderings, her choice of duty to her father rather than duty to him. Angered by her opposition, he began to doubt even her love, or to count that love a poor and paltry thing; the love that can consider another rather than the beloved one; the love so closely allied with remorse that it almost ceases to be love.

A long letter from Edith Champion, which reached him during his last days at the Rosary, seemed to accentuate Hester's coldness. Edith's letter was glowing with hopeful love. Her year of widowhood was drawing towards its close. June would soon be here, and then, if he still cared for her, their new life might begin. He had never been absent from her thoughts during her exile. The winter had seemed very long, but the dawn of spring meant the dawn of hope.

The letter claimed him, and, in his present mood, he had no desire to dispute that claim. The pale sweet face which looked at him in mute agony on that last March morning had lost its power to move him.

"You will come back to me, Gerard?" she entreated, clinging to him in a farewell embrace.

"Perhaps! Who knows if I may live long enough to see you and England again? You have made your choice, Hester. The future must take care of itself. In any case your welfare is provided for. I have taken care of all material matters—for you and yours."

That was all. There was no tender allusion to that new obligation which the summer was to bring upon Hester and upon him. His heart was full of a sullen anger against this woman whose sacrifice just stopped short of blind obedience.

Her heart turned to ice at this cold reply. Womanly pride, the pride of a deeply injured woman, rose up against him at this last moment. Her arms dropped from his neck. The wan

cheek that had been pressed against his was
turned away. She followed him silently into the
hall, and stood by in silence while he was being
helped on with his fur-lined coat, and saw him
step into the snug little brougham, with the
dumb, tearless agony of a leaden despair. He
looked out of the carriage window and waved her
a smiling good-bye. The smile hurt her more
than his harshest words could have done.

CHAPTER II.

"SING WHILE HE MAY, MAN HATH NO LONG DELIGHT."

GERARD and his companion started for the South in the *train de luxe* that left Charing Cross early in the forenoon. A sunlit passage across the Channel, a day of cigar-smoking and newspaper-reading, and brief intermittent slumbers, into which they sank, not from sleepiness, but from sheer weariness and vacuity: an evening at piquet, played under the vacillating light of a couple of reading-lamps, while the train rushed southward: and then a long weary night in which the same rushing sound, the same incessant oscillation, mixed itself with every dream, while now and again the sudden thunder of a passing train startled the dreamer with some strange image

conjured instantaneously out of the distorted
dream-world.

Gerard's spirits had been variable all through
the long day and evening, now breaking out into
gaiety, anon sinking into gloom. His strongest
feeling was a sense of relief. He had escaped
from a life that had been gradually growing
abhorrent to him. He had escaped from the
house of melancholy, from the atmosphere of
undying remorse. Most of all, he had escaped
from the presence of Nicholas Davenport—that
living spectre, the dismal simulacrum of humanity,
the perpetual reminder of old age, disease, and
death; the mindless automaton whose vicinity
made life hideous.

"If duty is more to her than love she must find
happiness in doing her duty," he said to himself
again and again, while his thoughts set themselves to the rhythmical beat of the engine.
"She must find happiness—doing her duty!"
With every thud those words repeated themselves.

He had done his duty by her, he told himself.
He had given her the option, and she had decided.
Her lover or her father? She had chosen to stand

by the earlier tie. Obstinately, needlessly, in opposition to all reason, she had sacrificed herself to the father whose only claim upon her love at the best had been a father's name. She had chosen.

Yes, he had done his duty. Hurried although his flight from England had been, eager as he was to plunge into new scenes, to wash the bitter taste of memory out of his mouth with the waters of novelty, he had taken every step necessary to ensure Hester Davenport's material prosperity. His last act before leaving London had been to execute a deed of trust which provided for her. She would be a rich woman all the days of her life—a very rich woman—able to enjoy all that wealth can offer of splendour, luxury, variety, the world's esteem, long after he would be inurned in bronze or marble, a handful of mindless dust. She had known the sharp sting of poverty all through the fairest years of her youth, and would be the better able to appreciate the privileges of wealth. He told himself that he could afford to think of her without one remorseful pang; yet he did not so think in the enforced vacuity of long sleepless hours, cramped, with aching limbs, in his narrow berth. The pathetic face, the imploring eyes, haunted him.

He thought of the infinite consolations of her life—a life not measured, like his miserable existence, within the narrow limits of a year or two. If she was alone now, alone with that sad phantasm of mindless humanity, she would have a new companion before very long—the sweetest, tenderest companion woman's life can know—the child who in every attribute recalls all that was best and dearest in the father.

" If I had stayed with her to the end our parting must have come all the same," he told himself, " and why should I sacrifice my poor remnant of life to the horror of an association that agonises me ? One little year, perhaps, at the best. Only a year. Am I a wretch because I try to make the most of that last year ? "

He looked at Justin Jermyn, sleeping on the other side of the carriage, the image of placid repose ; his breathing as regular as an infant's ; his complexion delicately fair in the lamplight ; his parted lips rosy as the lips of a child.

" *There* is enjoyment of life," mused Gerard, " and yet I don't believe that man ever had an

unselfish thought, or would hesitate at the com-
mission of the darkest crime, if crime could make
life pleasanter to him."

He remembered how Jermyn had pushed him
on to his alliance with Hester, and how Jermyn
had urged him to sever the tie directly it became
irksome—a man who perhaps had done very little
evil on his own account, who had neither robbed
the widow and orphan nor murdered his friend,
but who went about the world giving evil advice
lightly, with a graceful carelessness, a perpetual
happy-go-lucky air which minimised the wrong-
fulness in every transaction, and made so airy a
jest of virtue that vice seemed non-existent. And,
after all, when a man has filed down his beliefs
to absolute materialism, when he says of that
microcosm, himself, "Thou art as the beasts that
perish," it becomes very hard to define vice and
virtue.

In the grey dawn Gerard envied his Mentor
that childlike slumber, that perfect complacency
and content with life. And then what physical
advantages the man had! Lungs sound as a bell;
muscles which no exercise could tire—on the
river, in the gymnasium, on tennis-court or golf-

links alike inimitable. Yes, that was the glory of life—a mind without sense of good and evil; a body endowed with health and strength, and with the promise of long life in every organ and every limb. Better than millions; better than that plethora of gold which seemed a mockery to the man whose days were numbered.

Gerard pondered on the months that he had wasted in the cottage by the river, living as a man might live whose income was under a thousand a year; he who had the spending of nearly a hundred thousand in the twelve months if he chose; he whose duty it was, knowing himself doomed to early death, to riot in gold, to wallow in the waters of Pactolus, to melt pearls of price in his wine, to achieve some mad extravagance— some folly which should be remembered when he was dust—almost every day of his life.

For fame he had done nothing. Granted that he had furnished a house which in every detail testified to lavish expenditure and superior taste ; but do not the wool-growers of Australia and the petroleum merchants of America as much as that? Clever as he fancied himself, he had made no new departure. He had given *recherché* luncheons, and had succeeded in having his hospitality spoken of as "the Hillersdon *table d'hôte*" by the witlings of his circle, mostly, perhaps, by those whom he did not entertain. He had bought some of the costliest books from famous collections lately brought to the hammer. He had patronised some rising artists, eccentrics of the French and Belgian schools; had bought statues, and had given exorbitant sums for carriage horses which he rarely used, and for a Park hack which he rode so seldom that every ride had been a narrow escape of sudden death. And in works of beneficence—what was the record there? He had given freely, given carelessly and unquestioningly, given to all who asked, tossing the letters of appeal from Charities or from individuals to his secretary, with the order to send a cheque "for whatever you think fit." It may be that gold distributed thus unthinkingly had done as much harm as it had done good, had fed the professional begging-letter writer, and encouraged the drunken hanger-on of Fortune. He had devoted his wealth to no great work for the public good. He had dedicated no recreation-ground, no park or lawn, to the joyless dwellers in the seething slums. He had built no wholesome and airy habitations to replace the loathsome dens of Bethnal Green or Bermondsey. No; he had done very little with his money; he, who when penniless had pondered so often on the potentialities of wealth, and had wondered at the sorry use the average millionaire makes of his golden opportunities! He, Gerard Hillersdon, man of the world, thinker, dreamer, fully abreast with all the newest ideas, felt that his career up to this point had been a failure. And the time that remained to him for achievement was so short! He was oppressed by a sense of hurry, an eagerness to enjoy, which kept his blood at fever-point. How slow was this so-called express: how uncomfortable this *train de luxe*!

While the glamour of a passionate love had lasted that tranquil existence by the river had been perfect happiness; but now, by a strange perversity of mind, he looked back upon the placid monotony of those days with a feeling that was akin to disgust. It was not that he could contemplate Hester's image without tenderness; but between the fair young face and his picture of the Rosary there came an image of horror—the face and form of the man whose shattered brain was in some wise his work. He forgot all that he had enjoyed of exquisite bliss—the dual joys of a supreme and unselfish love—in the nearer memory of that one hideous night, in the painful associations of that after time when Hester's heart had been divided between love and duty.

No train could travel fast enough to carry him away from those memories. They were at Monte Carlo in the golden light of afternoon. Only yesterday they had breakfasted at the London Métropole in the grey gloom of an English March. To-day they were taking afternoon-tea on a wide balcony overlooking the sunlit Mediterranean, Monaco's promontory with its twin towers, and all the theatrical gardens and turrets, stucco pinnacles, flower-decked terraces, steps and balustrades of Monte Carlo.

They were to stay here for a few days, as long as the place amused them, and then they were to go to Florence, rapidly or by easy stages, as the spirit moved them. Jermyn's spirits were too equable to be brightened by the change from London greyness to this fairy-land of

Europe, but he flung back his head with a gay laugh and sniffed the balmy air with sensuous appreciation.

"What a sensible man your doctor was to send you to the South," he exclaimed, "and what a sensible man you were to invite me to be your travelling companion."

"I should have been bored to death if I had come alone," answered Gerard, laughingly, "and I really think you are the one man whose society suits me best—though I have the most despicable opinion of your morals."

"My dear Hillersdon, I never set up for having any morals. I don't know what morals mean. There are certain things that I wouldn't do, because no man can do them and hold his head up in society. I wouldn't cheat at cards, for instance, or open another man's letter. Between men there is a kind of honesty which must be observed, or society couldn't hold together. Between men and women : well, I think you must have found out long before you met me that the weaker sex is outside the laws of honour, and that a man who would rather perish than *sauter la coupe* at whist or introduce an

extraneous king at écarté thinks it a bagatelle
to trick a woman out of her reputation. Yet,
after all, in the net result of life I believe
women have the best of it; and for every one
whom we lead astray there are two who fatten
upon our destruction, a fact which you may see
exemplified in this charming place."

They were at a brand new hotel, a white
walled palace built on a height commanding
sea and shore. La Condamine lay in a sunny
hollow below them, a concatenation of white villas
and red roofs and narrow gardens, balconies and
trellises brimming over with roses, the rich
purple masses of the Bougainvilliers conspicuous
above wall and gable, hedges of pink and scarlet
geranium, an avalanche of azaleas pouring down
the hill to the lapis blue of the sea. The hotel
was so new that it seemed to have been built
and furnished expressly for Mr. Hillersdon's
occupation. The courtly manager assured him
that the suite of rooms reserved for him had
never been inhabited. They were on the second
floor, and consisted of ante-room, saloon, and
dining-room, bedrooms and bathroom, all up-
holstered in the same silvery greys and greens,

with artistic touches of warmer colour here and there, to accentuate the prevailing coolness. A marble loggia extended the whole length of the windows, and in this balmy climate the loggia was the most delightful spot in which to live.

Gerard and his companion strolled down to the casino after their eight o'clock dinner. The season was nearly over, and there was ample space for moving about in the gaudy mauresque rooms, but the players gathered thickly round the tables, under the vivid light concentrated on the green cloth; and there were plenty of people in the trente et quarante room, a higher class perhaps than are to be found in the height of the season, when the idle and the curious surge in and out and peer and watch and whisper, to the annoyance of the players who mean business and nothing else.

For Gerard since his accession to fortune play had but little charm. While he was still poor he had hankered after the feverish delights of the baccarat table, and had frequented clubs where play ran high, venturing small stakes, which when smallest were more than he could afford to lose—but now that loss or gain signified nothing to him he needed some stimulus from without to give a flavour to play.

He found that stimulus for the moment in the very atmosphere of the trente et quarante room, where some of the handsomest women and some of the quickest witted men in Paris crowded round the tables and elbowed him as he leant forward to deposit his stakes. He played very carelessly, sometimes letting his winnings lie on the table till they were trebled and quadrupled before the inexorable rake swept them away, sometimes putting aside his gains in a little heap of gold and notes, which some of those lovely Parisian eyes watched covetously. He was more interested in the people at the table than in the game. It surprised him to see how many of these people exchanged greetings with Justin Jermyn, who had elbowed his way to the front, and was playing with small stakes in a light casual way. His careless nods, his sharp sudden handshakes indicated considerable intimacy with those of the players by whom he was greeted. The beautiful women smiled at him with an air of patronage, and he was equally patronising to the keen-eyed men. A little ripple

of low laughter, a flutter of whispers went round
the table, quieted only by the authoritative hush
of the dealer.

Gerard, after playing languidly for half an
hour, pocketed his little heap of gold—the notes
having been swept away by the inexorable rake,
and gave himself up to observation of the players.
How beautiful some of those faces were—and
most of them how wicked! Here the bright
black eyes and tilted nose of the soubrette type,
there a Roman profile, with eyes and hair like
Erebus, and there again a Saxon beauty with
milky skin, pale eyes, and yellow hair. They
all hailed from Paris these syrens, Lutetia being
the paradise and happy hunting-ground of their
kind; but they were of various nationalities,
including a hard-eyed and hard-headed English-
woman, with a plain face and a perfect figure,
in a close-fitting tailor gown, severe and un-
compromising amongst the sumptuous demi-
toilettes of sister syrens. This lady was reputed
to be richer than any other of the feminine
gamesters, and was further reported to have
refused her hand in marriage to a British Duke.
But there was one face at the trente et quarante

table which interested Gerard Hillersdon more
than all this cosmopolitan beauty, the one only
face which wore the typical expression of the
gambler, a face haggard with intensity, pinched
and worn with inward fever. It was the face of a
small elderly woman, who sat at the end of the
table near the dealer, and who from time to time
consulted a perforated card, upon which she
marked the progress of the game; a small face,
with delicate aquiline features, thin lips, silvered
hair, and dark eyes that seemed too large for the
pinched face. There was that in the careless
attire, the shabby little black lace hat, of a
fashion of four or five years ago, the Spanish
lace shawl hanging in slovenly folds over one
shoulder, ragged and rusty with long wear, the
greasy black silk gown, which told of woman-
hood that had done with womanly graces, and
had sacrificed to one darling vice all the small
follies, caprices, and extravagances of the sex.
Gerard became more interested in this one
player than in the fortunes of the table, so
absorbed indeed that Jermyn had to touch his
shoulder twice before he could attract his
attention.

"It is close upon eleven o'clock," said Jermyn, "and the rooms shut at eleven. What are we to do with the rest of the evening? There are plenty of people here whom I know. Shall I invite a few of them, the most amusing, to your rooms?"

"By all means. Ask them to supper. Let us make believe that the world is nearly two centuries younger, that we are living in the Regency, and that Philip of Orleans is our boon companion. Your follies cannot be too foolish nor your dissipation too wild for my humour. Let this Rock be our Brocken, and invite all the handsome witches of your acquaintance."

"What even the poor pretty girl with the red mouse in her mouth? And Marguerite; what of Marguerite?"

Gerard winced at the allusion.

"My Marguerite has chosen her destiny," he said. "If she were like Goethe's Gretchen she would have chosen differently. Love would have been all in all with her."

Gerard strolled out of the rooms alone, while Jermyn passed quickly and quietly from group to group and briefly whispered his invitations, which were accepted with a nod or a smile. The people to whom these invitations were given belonged to a class which might adopt the motto of a certain great border clan for their own. *Je suis prêt!* Always ready for the chances of the moment, always ready to be entertained at anybody else's expense, be the entertainer a Watts or a Pullinger, ripe for Portland, or a typical vulgarian of the Hibernian-American type; always ready for ortolans and champagne, for turtle and white-bait, for a saturnalia on a house-boat at Henley, or an orgie at the Continental. Always ready: ready as the vultures are ready, for dead hero or dead dog, when the scent of the carrion is wafted to them from afar off on the wings of the wind.

Gerard strolled slowly, very slowly, up the hill to the big brand new caravansary where the electric light gave something of that elfin brilliancy which suggests the halls of Eblis. Slowly as he walked up that brief ascent, carefully graduated by artful windings for the footsteps of the weak-lunged, he was breathless when he arrived in the vestibule, and had to rest for a few minutes before he could give his orders to the manager.

"A supper—all that there is of the best—for, say, a party of twenty. Do all you can in fifteen minutes. You can give us those little green oysters, and plenty of them. Chateau Yquem, Clos Vougeot. For champagne, well, Heidsec or G. H. Mumm—but I leave the details to you and my friend Mr. Jermyn. Be sure there are lights and flowers in the loggia. And if you can get us any music worth hearing so much the better."

"There are the Neapolitan singers, monsieur; I dare say we can find them."

"*Funicoli, funicola*, I suppose. *C'est connu*, but it will be better than nothing."

Before the stroke of midnight he was sitting at a supper table crowded with roses and azaleas, stephanotis and lilies of the valley, and surrounded with the fine flower of the Parisian demi-monde. What a fairy ring of bright eyes and jewels as dazzling, of eccentric and exquisite toilettes, the very newest colours in fashion's ever-changing rainbow; a general abandonment to the delight of the hour; not vicious—for even sinners are not always bent on sin—but unrestrained. What

light laughter; what frank, joyous jesting; airy
sentences which in that particular environment
sounded like epigrams, but which would seem
witless in print; lightest talk of the Paris
theatres, the dramas that had succeeded, Heaven
knows why, the brilliant comedies which had
gone out in the foul smoke of ridicule, failure,
and disappointment; the intrigues in the great
world and the half-world; the undiscovered
crimes; the impending disasters. These careless
speakers discussed everything, and decided everything, from dynasties to dressmakers.

Gerard Hillersdon relished that light touch-
and-go of the Celtic intellect, trained to folly,
but folly spiced with wit. He had tried pleasure
in London, and had found it dull and dreary.
The ladies he met at the Small Hours were
mostly so intent upon being ladies that they
forgot to be amusing. The days were past of
that fair *mauvaise-langue* who charmed the
peerage, and whose sturdy British bon-mots were
circulated over civilised Europe, plagiarised in
Paris, and appropriated in Vienna. He had
sought wild gaiety, and he had found decent
dulness. Here, the spirit of fun was not wanting,

and the joyous laughter of his guests was loud
enough to drown the voices of the Neapolitans
in the loggia, yea, even the twanging of their
guitars. And by and by the Neapolitans were
pushed into a corner, and bidden to twang only
waltzes, and those loveliest women in Paris were
revolving in rythmical movement in the arms of
the keen, clever men, of no particular profession,
who constituted their travelling body-guard.
Gerard took two or three turns with a lovely
German girl, with a creamy complexion and
innocent blue eyes, who had done little more
than smile sweetly upon the contest of wit and
animal spirits, and who was said to have *rincé*
(Anglice, beggared) one of the wealthiest Jew
bankers of Frankfort.

He could not stand more than those two or
three gentle turns to a slow three-time waltz, and
he sat in the loggia breathless and exhausted,
while the fair Löttchen tripped away to her
friends and told them that it was finished with
yonder crétin, who would very soon find his way
to the Boulanger.

"*En attendant,* he has given us a capital
supper," replied a lady who was called Madme.

la Marquise in society, but plain Jeannette Foy
in all legal documents. "I hope he will leave
us money for mourning. *Moi, je me trouve
ravissante en noir!*"

Gerard enjoyed the restful solitude of the
loggia for half an hour, the fun within having
waxed fast and furious, and his guests being
somewhat oblivious of his existence. Yes, it was
a wild whirl of mirthful abandonment which
verily suggested the witches' dance upon the
haunted hills. There were little spurts of
malignity now and again from the lips of beauty,
which were like the red mouse that dropped out
of the rosy girlish mouth. Gerard watched this
pandemonium from the cool seclusion of the
loggia, while the Neapolitans played languidly,
and even dozed over their guitars, with an
occasional automatic twang. Yes, it was like a
witches' Sabbath, or like a dance of wicked spirits
in the halls of Eblis. Thank Heaven, in that
gaudy, many-coloured crowd, amidst the flashing
of diamonds and waving of plumed fans, and
flutter of silk and lace, there was no ghastly warning vision of his absent love, that Hester whom
he had loved so fondly and left so heartlessly.

He pictured her in the wind-swept garden by the river, where the March skies were grey and gloomy, and the hyacinths were shivering in the nipping air. Why was she not with him here? Why was she not sitting by his side, they two alone, looking out over the sleeping town, the colony of white villas in the crescent-shaped hollow, the old, old steep-roofed houses and twin-towered cathedral, yonder on the jutting rock? Why were they not together in the star-shine of the balmy night; here, as they had been on the starlit river last year, all in all to each other, knowing no duty, no religion, no law but to adore each other? It was her own fault that they were parted. Had she been with him, these ribald revellers would not have been there. He would have found enough happiness in her sweet society. He had never changed to her. It was she who had changed to him.

He was glad to have escaped from that atmosphere of remorse, glad to be on his way to his first love, glad most of all to be in this fairer world, by the side of the sea of deathless memories, glad to be under these brighter stars. Even folly was pleasant to him as a relief from too much thought. When his new acquaintances of the night remembered his existence so far as to come out into the loggia to take leave, in the faint roseate glow of approaching day, he invited the fairest and wittiest among them to breakfast with him.

"Not to-morrow, but to-day," he said; "Jermyn must devise new pleasures for us—picnics, excursions, by sea or mountain. I mean my brief stay here to be all holiday—if you will help me."

He held the fair Bavarian's hand in his, while the bright black eyes and white teeth of the pug-nosed Comtesse Rigolboche smiled down upon him.

"I had booked my place in the *train de luxe* for to-morrow," said Rigolboche, "but I'll change the date and stay here as long as you do. We'll all help you to conjugate the verb *rigoler*. *Rigolons, rigolez.*"

The other voices took up the word, and the revellers departed to a chorus of "Rigolons, rigolez."

Mr. Jermyn was equal to the occasion. He ordered *dejeuners* and dinners. He elicited the

talents of the *chef*, he taxed the resources of the
well-found hotel. He kept the telegraph wires
employed between Monte Carlo and Nice, Mar-
seilles, and Paris, and choicest dainties were
expressed along the line. Alternating with
messages that involved life and health, fortune,
all that is gravest in the destiny of man, flew
orders for Perigord pies or monster lobsters,
Chasselas grapes, Alpine strawberries, oysters,
ortolans, quails. Everything Jermýn touched
was successful, and that week at Monte Carlo
was a triumph of gourmandise and wild amuse-
ment. The hills echoed with the songs of the
revellers; the sea waves danced to the music of
their laughter as they sailed round the point of
Rocque Brune, or lay becalmed in the sheltered
Gulf of Ospedaletti. The weather was exquisite
—that perfect atmosphere of spring-time on the
Riviera which makes one forget that those lovely
shores have ever been visited by mistral and
sirocco, rain and sleet. It was earthquake
weather, Justin Jermyn said, remembering how
fair had been that February which was startled
by an appalling shock of earthquake. He told
them that this glad, beautiful shore was pre-

paring itself for just such another convulsion, but the joyous band laughed him to scorn.

"If a great pit were to open in this mountain and swallow us all alive I should not care," said Rigolboche, emptying her glass with a piquant turn of her wrist and small neat hand. "*J'ai vecu.* I have lived my life."

Hillersdon sighed. How lightly this woman thought of life, while he counted each vanishing hour, and clung with longing desire to the remnant of his days, and could not resign himself to the inevitable end, could not bring himself to say, "I have lived, and am content to die."

Löttchen, the Bavarian girl, had attached herself to him with devotion since that first waltz when she had spoken of him with such brutal scorn. She had gone from scorn to pity, and pity had deepened into love. In all their revellings she tried to be near him, hung upon his footsteps, sought his society. Her soft, clinging ways touched his heart, but that heart was cold to all her charms. She was no more to him than a pretty child by the roadside, holding up a handful of flowers as his carriage drove by.

Rigolboche, too, the reckless and brilliant

Rigolboche, who spent more money and who owed more than any lady of her set, tried all the keenest weapons of her wit upon the *deux-fois* millionaire—*des millions sterlings, bien entendu*—but the wit of the Parisienne had no more power to fascinate Gerard Hillersdon than the blonde loveliness of the Bavarian. It may be that he had outlived the power of loving; that in his intensified anxiety for his own life all other personalities had become indifferent. If he was looking forward eagerly to reunion with Edith Champion it was because in that reunion he hoped to recover the freshness of his vanished youth, to become once again hopeful and full of energy, as in the days that were gone.

The spirits which Jermyn had assembled served to amuse the man who felt himself doomed, and that was much. That circle of bright faces shut out the dark images which were wont to press round him when he was alone. That festal companionship made thought impossible; and when the night of revelry ended, mostly on the edge of day, Gerard Hillersdon was so thoroughly wearied that he slept more soundly than he had done for a long time.

There was pleasure, too, in the knowledge that he was spending his money. The more lavish the entertainment, the more extravagant the feast, the better was he pleased. Rarely had the boatmen of la Condamine fared as they fared with him. It was his delight to see them rioting on the surplus of the banquet, devouring quails at a mouthful, swilling the costliest wines, digging their rude clasp-knives into pies that had come by express train from Chevet. He flung gold pieces about with the lavish bounty of an Indian Rajah. The waiters at the hotel fawned upon him as if he had been an emperor; the manager addressed him in hushed accents as if he had been a god.

He spent an hour at the rooms every evening. He liked to see his syrens play, and he supplied them with the funds for their ventures at the trente et quarante tables. For his own part he played no more after the first evening. The game did not interest him, but the players did. So he moved about quietly, or stood in the background, and watched the faces in the lamp-light.

The little elderly woman with the dark

haggard eyes was generally in the same place near the dealer, her bonnet always badly put on and carelessly tied, her lean, ungloved hands not conspicuously clean. Gerard derived a sinister pleasure from his observations of this woman. She was a study in morbid anatomy. All the forces of her being were concentrated upon the card-table. There were nights when she was radiant, glorified, as if some supernal lamp were burning behind the dull olive complexion, and flashing through the dark Italian eyes. There were other nights when her face had a marble fixity, which would have been like death had not the unceasing movement of the anxious eyes made that marble mask more awful than death. Gerard found after a time that this woman was conscious of being observed, that, in spite of the concentration of all her faculties upon the gaming table, she had a restlessness under scrutiny, a nervous apprehension which showed itself from time to time in birdlike glances in his direction, or in an angry movement of the head or shoulders. He tried, perceiving this, to disguise his interest, and watched her furtively, hoping to escape observation. He had noted that on the thin black cord on which her *pince-nez* hung she had one of those horn-shaped corals which the Italian peasant deems a charm against the evil eye, and he had noted how as he passed near her on two or three occasions she had clutched this talisman in her skinny fingers, automatically, as if moved by an instinct of self-defence.

It was his last night at Monte Carlo, and the eve of a water picnic which was to signalise his departure, and was to be the bouquet in the series of entertainments organised by Justin Jermyn. He had spent half an hour at a jeweller's on the hill, and had chosen farewell gifts for the syrens, including a superb diamond hoop for the slim round wrist of Löttchen, in whose eyes he had seen tears of real tenderness yesterday when a violent access of his cough had left him speechless and exhausted. For every tear he would give her a diamond of purest water, and yet would think her tears poorly recompensed.

He went down to the rooms for the last time that season. Would he ever see those rooms

again, he wondered, at any season? Were not
all seasons fast closing for him: or would
science, aided by wealth, patch up these feeble
lungs of his, and spin out the frail thread of
existence yet a few more years in the summer
lands of earth? He would go anywhere; to
the South Seas, to the West Indies, to the
Himalayas; anywhere only to live; and he told
himself that Edith Champion would deem no
land a place of exile where they two could
live together. She had no other ties, no superior
claim of duty, or exaggerated filial love. Her
sacrifice to her husband's manes and to society's
good opinion had been made. Three-quarters
of her year of widowhood were spent, and when
she saw what need he had of a wife's protecting
companionship, she would doubtless waive the
remnant of that ceremonial year, and marry him
off-hand, at the Florentine Legation.

The thought of her was in his mind to-night.
He had enjoyed his week of folly; the sound
of the jester's bells had been sweet in his ear;
but he was weary of that silvery jingle, and
he looked forward with pleasure to the sober
luxuries and splendours of his life with Edith.

He was in treaty, through Justin Jermyn, for the *Jersey Lily*, one of the finest yachts at Nice, and with this yacht he and his wife would make a tour of all the fairest ports of the Mediterranean—lingering or hastening as caprice prompted.

The shabby little woman was at her post as usual, and one furtive glance at her face told Gerard that luck had been against her. She had the rigid, death-like look he knew so well. He stood on the opposite side of the table watching her—across the burly shoulders of an English bookmaker, returning from a race-meeting in the Roman Campagna, and loud in his denunciation of the pari-mutuel system. Her bad luck continued. Stake after stake—ventures which had dwindled to the minimum morsel of gold—were swept away by the inexorable rake, until she sat with clasped hands, watching and not playing; too well known an habituée to be asked to make way for the players. The officials knew her ways, and that after sitting statue-like during two or three deals she would rise slowly, as one awakening from a painful dream, and walk quietly away—to reappear the following night with money obtained none knew how.

Gerard felt in his breast pocket for a bundle of notes, and went round the table towards the back of the lady's chair, intending to push the money quietly into her hand, and to vanish before she had recovered from her surprise at his action; but his intention was frustrated, for as his hand brushed against her shoulder she started up suddenly as if she had been stung, and turned upon him with eyes that burnt like coals of fire in her pallid face. The rapidity of her movement, and that burning gaze disconcerted him. He drew back in confusion.

The lady advanced upon him as he retreated, until they were at some distance from the tables, away from the glare of the lamps. Then she stopped, fixing him with her fiery eyes.

"You do not appear to be an ardent gambler, monsieur," she said.

"No, madame, I am not a gambler. Trente et quarante is utterly without interest for me."

"Why then do you haunt these rooms?"

"I come to observe others, and to be amused."

"Amused by evil passions which you do not

share, amused as devils are amused with the vices and passions of humanity. Do you not know that your presence here is odious, that your glances bring misfortune wherever they rest?"

"I do not know why that should be. I have no malicious intention. I am only a looker-on."

"So is death a looker-on at the game of life, knowing that sooner or later he must win. Your presence here is fatal, for there is death in your face; and since this room was not built for idle observers, but for business-like players, you will be doing everybody a favour by absenting yourself in future. I am assured that I have expressed the desire of the whole assembly."

She made him a sweeping curtsey, drew her ragged shawl about her shoulders, and passed him on her way to the door. He stood with his packet of notes still in his hand, looking after her dumbly.

Yet one more voice to remind him of approaching doom.

CHAPTER III.

"SOME LITTLE SOUND OF UNREGARDED TEARS."

THE farewell festival had been arranged by
Justin Jermyn with especial care. He had
secured the *Jersey Lily*, the yacht for which
Gerard hankered. Her owner, a rich commercial
man, was tired of his plaything, and was glad to
sell her to a purchaser who did not drive a hard
bargain. The yacht, a fine sailer, with auxiliary
steam, was in full working order, and Gerard's
first cruise was to be this water picnic. For
music Mr. Jermyn was no longer content with
itinerant Neapolitans. He had engaged some
of the best performers at the famous concerts in
the Casino. But his greatest success was with
the floral decorations. In these he had surpassed
himself, while he had ransacked the Algerian
shops on the hill for Oriental fabrics, gay with

gold and colour, and glittering with morsels of looking-glass, to drape cabins and poop.

March was drawing to an end, and the weather was delicious, the April summer of the South, weather that would make even the dull flats of Essex or Norfolk enchanting, but which over that lovely land breathes an intoxicating influence, giving to age the gladness of youth, to weakness the pride of strength.

Lunch was over, and the yacht was lying to in the roadstead of Antibes. Some of the more enterprising of the party had been rowed ashore, and had set out on a pilgrimage to the church on the height—the church with its curious votive pictures, showing the Madonna's merciful interposition in all the perils of life, from a headlong fall out of a garret window to the overturning of a bicycle. Less active and exploring spirits were content to loll upon the deck, where low chairs and luxurious cushions invited slumberous ease. Fans were waving languidly in the golden light of afternoon, as if in time to the languid movement of the water fanned by the western wind. On one side stretched the long level seafront of Nice, with its line of white villas flashing in

the sunlight, far off to the rock crowned with
the lighthouse, and that jutting point which
shuts off the eastern sky towards Villefranche
and St. Jean.

Gerard was in high spirits. He wanted to
drain this cup of casual pleasures to the dregs.
He wanted to steep himself in the loveliness of
a coast which he might never look upon again.
It was bliss only to stand upon the deck as the
yacht lay at anchor and gaze upon that noble
range of hills, with varied lights and shadows
flitting across them, and that fair subtropical
Eden in the middle distance where the sapphire
sea kissed the low, level shore—a smiling land
of aloes and palms, orange groves, and grey-green
olive woods, with here and there white walls
and pinnacles gleaming amidst the green. It
was enough of bliss only to breathe such an
atmosphere and feel the inexpressible beauty
of earth.

" How happy you look to-day," said Löttchen,
watching the giver of the feast, as he leaned
against the gunwale, and looked dreamily across
the harbour to the rugged hill crowned with the
old-world city of Vence.

They two were alone in the bows, while the rest of the party were congregated in a joyous group in the stern, whence there came at intervals the deep, grave music of a 'cello, and the plaintive singing sound of violins in a serenade by Schubert. Pensive music, light laughter, floated towards these two on the summer wind. The German girl had followed Gerard when he withdrew from the noisy herd, leaving the inexhaustible Jermyn as its central figure, inspiring and sustaining the general mirth with that joyous laugh of his. Löttchen had stolen after Gerard, uninvited; but he was not so ungallant as to let her suppose that she was unwelcome.

"Yes," he said, "happy, but with only a sensuous happiness—the happiness of a well-cared-for cat basking and blinking in the sun ; happiness which vanishes at the first touch of thought. I am basking in the beauty of my Mother Earth, and if I think at all my only thought is that it would be sweet to live for ever —soulless, mindless, immortal—amidst such scenes as these; to live as the olives live on the slope of yonder hill, breathing the sweetness of this balmy air, feeling the glad warmth of this bounteous sun."

"It would be very dull after a week or two," said Löttchen, "and then what is life without love?"

"Life is much more than love. See how utterly happy children are in the enjoyment of the universe, and they know nothing of love—or at least of the passion to which you and I attach that name. To my fancy, this world would be perfect if we could be immortal and always children. That is the world of the elder gods. The deities of the rivers and the mountains, water-nymphs and wood-nymphs, what were they all but grown-up children, drunken with the sweetness and glory of life. But for us poor worms, whose every breath brings us nearer to the inevitable grave, what can this exquisite earth, with its infinite variety of loveliness, be but a passing show? We look, and long for its beauty; and even as we look it fades and melts into the dark. It is lovely still, but we are gone. Some one else will be watching those hills next year, some one as young as I am, and, like me, doomed to die in his youth."

Löttchen was silent. Tears were streaming down the fair cheek when Gerard turned to look at her.

She was lovely, engaging, sentimental—all that might charm a lover : but she left his heart cold as marble. Simply dressed in some soft fabric of purest white, and with a little white sailor hat perched on the artistic fluffiness of her flaxen hair, she looked the image of innocent girlhood, unspotted by the world. A man might easily forget all her history in such a moment as this, seeing the tears streaming from the large lucid eyes, the tender lips tremulous with emotion.

"Do not waste your tears or your sympathy upon me, Fräulein," Gerard said gently. "Weep only for the dying who do not grieve for themselves. I am utterly selfish, and am consumed by regret for my own doom."

"You might live longer, perhaps, if you were more careful of yourself," she said.

"There is no care that I would not take to live. It is only because I know the case is hopeless that I have given myself up. There is nothing left for me but concentrated pleasures.

There ought to be a melted pearl in every glass of wine I drink. And you have given me your pity—and pity from you has been sweet."

"Pity!" she echoed, with a deep sigh. "Well, call it pity, if you like."

He took a little velvet case from his pocket, and opened it in the sunlight. It seemed in that first flash of vivid light as if he had opened a box of sunshine more brilliant than those rays that danced upon the waves and turned the mountain clay to gold. The sunlight flashed back from the diamond circlet with rainbow glory, rose and emerald, violet, orange, blue.

"These diamonds are for your tears, Fräulein. Will you wear them sometimes as a souvenir of a dying man?"

She held out her arm as he unclasped the diamond circlet. It was a lovely arm, fair as alabaster, exquisitely modelled, dazzling to look upon as the soft white fabric fell away from it, and arm and wrist and tapering hand lay there, beautiful in the sunshine. There were those among Mdlle. Charlotte's admirers who declared that her arm and hand were her crowning beauty, and nearer the perfection of Greek sculpture than any other hand and arm in Paris.

Gerard clasped the diamond hoop upon the slender wrist, as it lay in languid grace upon the gunwale—clasped it without a word, and waited with calm indifference for the gush of gratitude which usually greets such gifts; but Löttchen's lips were speechless. She let her wrist lie for a minute or so where his fingers had lightly touched it as he clasped the bracelet, and then, with an inarticulate cry of grief or rage, she tore the snap asunder, and flung the flashing circlet into the sea.

"Do you think I care anything for your diamonds, when you care nothing for me?" she cried, and then ran away to the cabin, which had been made into a miniature zenana for Jermyn's bevy of sultanas, and emerged there-from no more till the boat returned to Monte Carlo in the moonlight, minus Gerard Hillersdon, who landed at Antibes, in order to be in time for the express for Genoa, which left Nice before sundown.

That little outbreak of Löttchen's touched him more than her beauty or her tears. "Queen

Guinevere in little," he said to himself, as he
looked after the retreating figure. "I suppose
women are alike all the world over. Dick
Steele best described the sex when he called
woman 'a beautiful romantic animal.' There is
a spice of romance in them all—even in the
most experienced demi-mondaine in Paris. Poor
Löttchen!"

He saw her no more, for she was not among
those who crowded to the side of the yacht to
see him drop into the dinghy. Her fair hand
was not among those which waved him farewell
as the row-boat moved swiftly towards the shore.

"*A riverdervi* next week at Florence," cried
Jermyn; and from the quay where he landed
Gerard looked back and saw the Fate-reader's
lissom figure sharply defined against the sky as
he stood on a raised portion of the deck, with
the syrens grouped about him.

It was in the sunset that Gerard bade farewell
to the western Riviera, and set his face towards
Genoa. Never can that lovely shore look
lovelier than just at that season of the year—
than just at that hour of dying day. Over all

the hills there lay the reflected flush from that crimson glory lingering yonder above the dark ridge of the Esterelles; over all the gardens, with their purple-red bloom of Bougainvilliers, their luxury of roses white and yellow, there hung the glamour of sunset; and over all the eastern sky spread an opaline splendour flecked with little rosy cloudlets, which looked like winged creatures full of exultant life, high up in that enchanted heaven. By every form of bay and inlet; by every delicate and gracious curve that the seashore can make, by rosy rock and shadowy olive wood, by every entrancing change from light to colour and from colour to light, the train sped onwards to the darkness of fortress-crowned Ventimiglia, where there was nearly half an hour's weariness and confusion, while Mr. Hillersdon's servant did battle with the Custom House officers, and transferred his master and his master's baggage to the Italian train. Then came a restless endeavour to slumber, more fatiguing than absolute wakefulness, and finally midnight and Genoa, where the traveller rested for a night.

He was in Florence on the following afternoon,

and the first idea with which that city inspired him was that he had left summer behind him. Some there are to whom the western Riviera is the supreme perfection of Italian landscape, and to whom all other spots seem cold and sombre as compared with that rich loveliness. Some there are who think that the chief glory of Italy is wanting when they have turned their back upon the Mediterranean, and that all that history, legend, and the fine arts can yield of interest and beauty is tame and dull compared with the magic of that sapphire sea, and the romantic variety of those rugged hills which look down upon it.

Gerard, walking through the streets of Florence on a grey March afternoon—March as chill and windy as he had ever known in Piccadilly—felt that a glamour had gone out of his life, and a warmth had left his veins. How dull the houses looked on the Lung'arno, palatial no doubt, all that the soul of an architect could desire; but are there not palatial houses in Piccadilly and Kensington? How grey the river, rushing over its weirs; how cold the colouring of the stone bridge; how bleak the snow line of the Apen-

nines. Tired as he was after the long journey
from Genoa, he had preferred to walk to his
destination, leaving servant and luggage to be
driven to the Hotel de la Ville, where his rooms
had been engaged for him.

He had given Mrs. Champion no notice of his
arrival. He wanted to take her by surprise, to
see in her face that he had lost nothing of the
love which was his a year ago. He had had his
caprice—had given all that was warmest and
best in his nature to another woman; and now
he wanted to take up the thread of life where
he had dropped it a year ago, when he followed
Hester Davenport across St. James' Park, and
felt the swift, sudden influence of love at first
sight. He wanted to love again, in the old,
reasonable, sober fashion; he wanted again to
feel the mild affection which had sustained his
interest in Edith Champion during the three
years of her wedded life.

Her house was on the side of the hill leading
to San Miniato—a villa in a delicious garden,
where the magnolia buds shone silver-white amid
the dark glossy leafage, and where broad beds
of flame-coloured tulips relieved the velvet

monotony of the lawn, while a tall hedge of pink peonies shivered in that scathing Florentine wind which has not been ill-described as an east wind blowing from the west.

It was a long walk from the station to that verdure-clothed hill on the southern side of the river, and Gerard was very weary when he arrived at the Villa Bel Visto, which overlooked the Boboli Gardens, and all the glory of Cupola and Campanile, far away to those fair hills northward of the city. On a sunny day the prospect would have cheered him with its beauty; but under this cold, grey British sky even dome and bell-tower lost something of their soothing influence, and Gerard regretted the sun-baked slopes above Monaco, where he seemed to have left summer behind him.

The gates stood wide open, and there were a good many smart carriages waiting in the semi-circular drive. The hall door was also open, while a distinctly British footman aired his idleness on the broad flight of marble steps, and looked with supercilious gaze upon the opposite hills. Gerard passed into the house uninterrogated, and found himself in a vestibule, from which several

doors opened. The light was dim, the atmosphere warm with the friendly glow of a wood
fire, and beyond, through half open doors, he
heard the subdued murmurings of voices, mostly
feminine, which suddenly dropped into silence
as he approached, silence broken by the flowing
phrases of a symphony, and then by a fine
baritone attacking the fashionable lament—
Vorrei morir. A majordomo, tall, handsome,
and Tuscan, stood near the lofty folding doors,
ready to announce visitors, and looked interrogatively at Mr. Hillersdon, who waited in silence
till the end of the song.

Mrs. Champion was evidently receiving—it
might be an afternoon party, or perhaps only her
" day." Her later letters had told him of a few
Florentine acquaintances, who dropped in occasionally to cheer her solitude; but he was unprepared for the crowd of well-dressed women and
distinguished-looking men amidst whom he found
himself when Tosti's pensive strain had died in a
prolonged diminuendo, and he allowed the major-
domo to announce him.

The afternoon light shone full upon a window
which occupied nearly one side of the spacious

drawing-room, and in this light Gerard saw Edith Champion standing in a group of elegant women of various nationalities—herself the handsomest of all, like an empress among her ladies of honour. She wore deepest black, but the heavy folds of the rich corded silk suggested grandeur rather than gloom, and the tulle coif, à la Marie Stuart, only gave a piquancy to the coronet of plaited hair which rose above her low, broad brow.

She started at the sound of her lover's name, and hurried to meet him.

"Welcome to Florence," she cried gaily, "though there is no one in the world whom I less expected to see. Have you only just come?"

"I have been in Florence less than an hour."

Her hand was in his, her lips were parted in a pleased smile, but as he came into the light of the wide window, he saw her expression change suddenly to a look of grieved surprise. He knew only too well what that look meant, though she gave no utterance to her thoughts. A year ago his friends frequently told him that he looked ill; but of late no one had told him so.

He had only read in their faces the evil augury which they saw in his face.

"I have come upon a festive occasion," he said, glancing round at the crowd.

"Oh, it is only my afternoon at home. People are so sociable in Florence. I have more people than usual to-day, because I let my friends know that Signor Amaldi had promised to sing. May I introduce him to you? No doubt you heard of him in London the season before last. He makes a sensation wherever he goes."

She beckoned to a small gentleman with fiery black eyes, and a large moustache, who lolled against the gaily draped piano, the centre of an admiring group, and the introduction was made.

Gerard knew enough Italian to compliment the singer in his own language without any grave offences against grammatical laws, and Signor Amaldi replied effusively, protesting that his musical gifts were poor things, mere wayside weeds, which he delighted to cast under the feet of the most gracious of English ladies.

Anon the piano was taken prisoner by a cadaverous German, with tawny hair, as closely cropped as if he were a fugitive from Portland,

and this gentleman expounded Chopin for the next half hour, amidst general inattention. The two English footmen were handing tea and chocolate, the women were whispering together in corners, and from an adjoining room came the tinkling of silver and glass at a liberally supplied buffet, at which a good many of the guests had congregated. But still those Hungarian war cries, those funereal wailings, shrieked and crashed, sobbed and sighed from the hard-ridden piano, while the German played on for his own pleasure and contentment, flinging up head and hands now and then in a sudden rapture during a bar of silence, and then swooping down upon the black notes like a bird of prey, and firing a volley of minor chords that startled the chatterers at the buffet and the whisperers in the corners of the salon.

During this musical interlude Edith and Gerard had time for a confidential talk.

"I hardly expected to find you so gay," he said.

"Surely you don't call this gaiety—a little music and a few pleasant people who have taken pity upon my solitude, and forced their acquaintance upon me. Florence is a gloomy place if one does not know people. There is so little to do after one has exhausted the galleries, and taken the three or four excursions which are *de rigueur*. But now you and the spring have come we can take all the old excursions together, bask in the sunshine at Fiesole, and buy perfumery from the dear old monks at the Certosa. I am so glad you have come."

"And yet you commanded me not to come until your year of mourning was ended. You refused to abate a single week."

" One is glad sometimes to have one's commands disobeyed. But tell me what made you come. Why did you disobey ? "

" Because my yearning for you was stronger than my obedience. I was utterly miserable, and I longed to see you."

"I am afraid you have been neglecting your health while I have been away," she said, looking at him earnestly.

" I have been ailing—but I am well now that I am with you. I look to you and Italy for healing. I have bought a yacht, and I am going to carry you off in it, as soon as the days are fair and long."

"That will not be till June, when my year of widowhood will be over."

"I am not going to wait for June. I am not going to wait for May. I snap my fingers at Mrs. Grundy. If you can give tea-parties you can marry me. My days of submission and waiting are over."

She laughed, and laid her hand gently upon his for a moment, and looked at him, and then sighed, while her eyes filled with sudden tears. She rose hurriedly and went away to talk to people who were leaving, and for the next quarter of an hour she was standing near the door bidding her friends good-bye.

Gerard moved about the rooms restlessly, but discovered no one whom he knew. He saw people looking at him with that quick furtive air in which good breeding struggles with curiosity. Suddenly he found himself in front of a large looking-glass, and saw himself from head to foot in the foreground of a group of well-dressed people, the women elegant and graceful, the men trim and well set-up.

How ghastly he looked, with his cadaverous cheeks and sunken eyes, doubtless a natural result of that wild week at Monte Carlo. How shabby, too, he to whom tailors' bills were of no consequence, he who in the days of his poverty had been the monitor of other young men, distinguished for the sober perfection of his toilet. Now, with his clothes hanging slackly upon his wasted frame, with the dust of travel still upon him, he looked an ugly blot upon the splendid elegance of Mrs. Champion's drawing-room. He went away hurriedly, slipping out by the dining-room door, unseen by Edith. He meant to have stayed and talked with her when the guests were gone, but a sudden disgust at life and at himself seized him as he contemplated his face and figure in the tall Venetian glass; and the thought of a *tête-à-tête* with his sweetheart was no longer pleasant to him.

He was with her next morning, before luncheon, and on this occasion the glass reflected at least a well-dressed man. He had taken particular pains with his toilet, and the pale grey *complet* and white silk tie had all the cool freshness of spring, while from the chief florist's in the Via Tornabuoni he carried a large nosegay of lilies of the valley and niphetos roses, as tribute to his mistress.

She welcomed him delightedly, and complimented him upon his improved appearance.

"You were really looking ill yesterday," she said, "a long dusty railway journey is so exhausting. This morning you have renewed your youth."

"And I mean to keep young, if I can. Am I over bold if I invite myself to your dejeuner?"

"I should think you very foolish if you waited for me to invite you. Come as often and as much as you can. Your knife and fork shall be laid for every meal. My sheep-dog will be on duty again this afternoon. She has been at Siena with some clerical friends, who insisted upon carrying her off to help them with her French and Italian—both of which, by the way, are odious."

"Are sheep-dogs wanted in Florence. I have been taught to think that Florentine society asks no questions."

"That shows your insular ignorance. Good society in Florence is like good society everywhere else."

"I understand. Severe virtue, tempered by Russian Princesses and their *cavaliere servente*."

They lunched *tête-à-tête*, under the protecting
eyes of the major-domo and the two British
footmen, in funereal liveries and powdered hair.
There was no opportunity for confidential talk,
nor did Gerard desire anything better than this
light, airy gossip about people they knew, and
the ways and works of their own particular world.
at home and on the Continent, from Royalties
downwards. He enjoyed this light talk. It
seemed to him that he had left passion, with its
accompaniment of sorrow, on the shores of the
Thames. To sit by the wood fire in Mrs.
Champion's salon, playing with her Russian
poodle, or turning over the newest French and
German books, or peeping into the dainty little
vellum-bound Florentine classics on the book-
table, while the lady sat by the window and
embroidered flame-coloured azalias on a ground
of sea-green satin, sufficed him. He felt restful,
and almost happy. He was as much at ease
with his *fiancée* as if they were old married
people. He told her of his yacht, and all its
luxuries and modern improvements. He talked
of those sunny Greek isles which they were to
visit together.

"I hope you will order some Greek gowns in your trousseau," he said; "I shall want you to dress like Sappho or Lesbia when we are at Cyprus or Corfu."

"I will wear anything you like, but I think a neat tailor gown made of white serge would be smarter and more shipshape than chiton or peplum."

The long afternoon was delightful to Gerard, and in spite of occasional anxious glances at her lover's face, Mrs. Champion seemed happy. It was pleasant to talk of that summer tour in the Greek Archipelago and the Golden Horn—how they were to go to this place or that to avoid undue heat; how they were to bask in the sun so long as his rays were agreeable; and how, before the days shortened again, they were to decide whether they would winter in Algiers or in Egypt, or whether it might not please them to travel further afield, to Ceylon, for instance, and that strange, gorgeous, antique world of Hindostan. There was all the restful consciousness of wealth underlying these day-dreams, the knowledge that the cost of things could make no difference.

Mrs. Gresham came buzzing in at tea-time, and after having endured her chatter about the Cathedral, the mosaics, the pictures, and the *table d'hôte* at Siena—including the wonder of wonders in having met Mrs. Rawdon Smith, of Chelmsford, and her daughter—for nearly an hour, Gerard took his leave, promising to return next day to luncheon, and to drive to Fiesole with Mrs. Champion and her cousin in the afternoon, provided the sun shone, which it had not done since his arrival in Florence.

He went back to his hotel, and dined in the solitude of a spacious salon overlooking the river and the Piazza. The candles were lighted within, clusters of candles in two tall candelabra, which brightened the table, but left the angles of the room in shadow. Outside the three large windows the evening was pale and grey, and in that soft greyness the lights on the old bridge and all along the quays shone golden.

Gerard, who was seldom able to eat alone, left his meal and went over to one of the windows. He opened the casement, and stood looking out over the marble bridge, and the rushing weir, and listening to the evening sounds of Florence,

with his elbows resting on the red velvet cushion
which covered the sill. First came the tattoo,
and the sound of soldiers marching in the piazza,
the trumpet-call repeated and then dying away
in the distance; and then the sonorous bell of
the church of All Saints filled the air, calling
the faithful to an evening service. It was Holy
Week, and there were services daily and nightly
in the church yonder—lighted altars, tapers
innumerable, throngs of worshippers.

The bell ceased after a while; and there was
no sound but the water rushing over the weir,
or occasional footsteps across the empty square.
Then the bell pealed out again, slow, solemn,
funereal, and from a cloister beside the church
issued the funeral train in all its Florentine
awfulness, hooded monks, flaming torches, darkly
shrouded bier. Gerard shut the casement with
angry suddenness, and went back to the deserted
dinner-table. He had dismissed all service.
The wine flasks and untasted dessert alone
remained in the light of the clustering candles.

The solitude within, the dismal tolling of the
bell without, the heavy colouring of the dimly
lighted room, weighed upon his spirits. He took

up his hat and went out. The streets would
be infinitely more agreeable than that spacious
emptiness within four walls.

The streets looked gay and bright in spite of
Holy Week. Lighted shop windows, people
passing to and fro; far better this than the
shadows of an empty room. There was neither
opera nor theatre open, or he would have sought
distraction of that kind. Great flaming posters
announced various performances of the lowest
music-hall type, and strictly British. From
these he recoiled. He passed the lighted portico
of a fashionable club, but did not test its
hospitality. He turned out of a broad street
into a narrow one—a short cut to the Piazza
Santa Maria Novella. A flare of yellow light
filled the further end of the street. Something
festal doubtless in defiance of Lent.

No, not festal. Again the black cowls, the
flaming torches, the darkly shrouded bier, and
suddenly from Santa Maria yonder the slow and
solemn bell. He turned on his heel, retraced his
steps quickly, emerged into the bright broad
street he had just left, only to meet another
procession. Again the cowls, the torches, and
the bier.

Florence was alive with funerals. There was nothing doing in the city, it seemed to him, but the burial of the dead. These funerals creeping through the night, mysterious under that uncertain flare of the torches, made death more awful. He hurried away towards the river, overtook an empty fly, and told the man to drive him to Mrs. Champion's villa, as fast as a Florentine horse would go. He felt a need of human companionship, of a warm, loving heart beating against his own, his own which seemed cold and dead as the hearts of those quiet sleepers who were being carried through the streets to-night.

"I am not fit to be alone," he told himself, as the light vehicle rattled over the bridge, to the Porta Romana. "I am full of vague apprehensions, like a child that has been frightened by his nurse. What is that strange fear of children, I wonder, that innate horror of something unexplained, indescribable? What but the hereditary dread of death, the infinite horror handed down from generation to generation, a fear which precedes knowledge, an instinct which antedates sense. In spite of Locke and all his school, there is one innate idea, if only one, and that is the fear of death. The wolf, the bear, the black man of the nurse's story, are all different images of that one unthinkable form."

He was ashamed of his own weakness, which had been so shaken by the passing of funerals in which he had no interest; but that tolling bell and those cowled monks had filled him with gloomy fancies. He thought of the plague-stricken city of the fourteenth century, and how Death held his court here while a few miles away in the garden in Doccia's dell light-hearted ladies listened to stories that have become part and parcel of the world's poesy, and then the song which he had heard yesterday in Mrs. Champion's drawing-room recurred to him—

> " ' Vorrei morir' quando tramonta il sole,
> Quando sui prato dormon le viole,
> Lieta farebbe a Dio l'alma ritorno,
> A primavera e sui morir del giorno."

Alas, and alas! would death be any sweeter to him because of a lovely sunset, or a woodland starred with primroses and banks purple with sweet-scented violets? What to him was spring or winter if he must die? Whether his last

breath went forth on the wings of the storm,
like Cromwell's and Napoleon's, or whether his
fading eyes turned their last look upon the
placid loveliness of a summer evening in a
pastoral country, could matter nothing to him.
Death meant the end—and death was unspeak-
ably cruel.

Mrs. Champion and her cousin were sauntering
in the garden after dinner, in the light of the
Easter moon, very tired of each other's society,
and even of the garden. Every life has these
dim evening hours, when there seems to be
nothing to live for.

" How good of you," cried Edith, recognising
her lover in the moonlight.

There was a fountain in a shallow marble basin
sending up its waters from the shadow of sur-
rounding foliage into the silvery light, and near
the fountain a broad marble bench with crimson
cushions spread upon it, where Mrs. Champion
was wont to sit. She seated herself on this bench
to-night, and, after a few words of commonplace,
Gerard took his place at her side, while Mrs.
Gresham discreetly returned to the drawing-
room, the poodle, and a Tauchnitz novel.

"You did not expect to see me so soon again, did you, Edith?"

"I did not expect—no—but I am so much the more glad."

"I could not live without you. I felt an aching wish to be with some one who loves me—to feel that I have still some hold upon warm human life."

And then he told her about the three funerals in the streets of Florence.

"Is it often so?" he asked. "Does Florence swarm with funerals?"

"My dear Gerard," she exclaimed laughingly. "Three! For a city of two hundred thousand inhabitants! Does that mean much? It is only the torchlight and the Brothers of the Misericordia that impressed you. How superior to anything one sees in England! So mediæval! so paintable! But don't let us talk of funerals."

"No, indeed! I am here to talk of something widely different. I want to talk of a wedding— our wedding, Edith. When is it to be?"

"Next June, if you like," she answered quietly.

"But I do not like. June is ages away. Who

knows if we may live to June. The monks may
be carrying us through the dark narrow streets
in the flare of their torches before June. I want
you to marry me to-morrow——"

"Gerard, in Holy Week!"

"What do I care for Holy Week? But if
you care, let us be married on Easter Monday.
We can start for Spezia after the ceremony, and
dine on board my yacht, in the loveliest harbour
in Europe. We can watch yonder moon shining
on the ghostly whiteness of the Carrara mountains, whiter, more picturesque, than those snow-
peaked Apennines."

"So soon!"

"And why not soon?" he urged impatiently.
"Edith, have I not waited long enough. Did I
not consume my soul in three long years of
waiting? Have I not wasted the best years of
my youth in silken dalliance, and frittered away
any talents I ever possessed upon the idlest of
love-letters, in which I was forbidden to talk of
love. Edith, I have been your slave—give me
something for my service before it is too late!"

"You are such a despondent lover," she said,
with a forced laugh.

" Despondent, no ; but I feel the need of your love. I feel that I am isolated, that I cannot live without some stronger nature than my own to lean upon, and that your character can supply all that is wanting in mine. We ought to be happy, Edith. We have youth, wealth, freedom, all the elements of happiness."

" Yes," she answered, with a faint sigh, " we ought to be happy."

" Let it be Monday, then. I will arrange all details."

" Easter Monday ! What a vulgar day for a wedding."

" Is it vulgar ? No matter, our marriage will be performed so quietly that hardly any one will know anything about it till they see the announcement in the *Times.*"

" Well, it must be as you like. You have been very good and devoted to me in all these years, and I don't think I shall be wanting in respect to my poor James, if I consent to marry you in April instead of June, though I dare say my sisters and people will talk. And as for my trousseau, I have plenty of gowns that will do well enough for your yacht. You must take me

to Palestine, Gerard. I have always longed to
see the Holy Land."

"You shall go wherever you like. You shall
be captain and commander of the *Jersey Lily*,"
he answered, bending down to kiss the beautiful
hand that moved in slow measure, waving a
feather fan. "She shall sail wherever you
order her."

They went into the house after this, and found
Rosa Gresham yawning over her novel, and the
poodle yawning on his bearskin rug. Nothing
could have been less romantic than this final
wooing; and if Gerard had not been too self-
absorbed to observe keenly, he must have been
struck by the contrast between Mrs. Champion's
manner to-night and in the old days in Hertford
Street.

They drove through the dust and shabbiness
of the outskirts of Florence next day, and up to
the hill-top, where Fiesole, the mother city, hangs
like an eagle's nest against a background of cloudless blue.

The day was steeped in sunshine and balmiest
air, and it was a happiness to escape from Lenten

Florence, with her solemn bells, to this winding road which went climbing upward by terraced gardens, and cypress hedges, and banks that glowed with tulips and anemonies, and fields where the young corn shone tender-green in the sunlight.

Here, while the horses rested, Mrs. Gresham went to explore the cathedral, leaving Edith and Gerard free to climb the steep path to the little grove on the top of the hill, where a steep flight of rugged stone steps lead up to the Franciscan convent and the church of St. Alessandro. Slowly, and very slowly, Gerard mounted that stony way, leaning on Edith Champion's arm, with sorely labouring breath. He stopped, breathless and exhausted, in front of an open shop, where an old man was mending shoes, who at once laid down his work, and brought out a chair for the tired Englishman. Edith entreated him to go no further, tried to persuade him that the view was quite as fine from the point they had reached as from the summit, but he persisted, and after resting for a few minutes, he tossed a five franc piece to the civil cobbler— leaving him overpowered at the largeness of

the donation—and went labouring up the few
remaining yards to the dusty little terrace, where
a group of noisy Germans and a group of equally
noisy Americans were expatiating upon the
panorama in front of them.

He sank panting upon the rough wooden
bench, and Edith sat by his side in silence,
holding his hand, which was cold and damp.

A deadly chill crept into her heart as she sat
there, hand in hand with the man whose life was
so soon to be joined with her life. The same
vague horror had crept over her two days ago,
when she had stood face to face with her lover
in the clear afternoon light, and had seen the
ravages which less than a year had made in his
countenance—had seen that which her fear told
her was the stamp of death.

CHAPTER IV.

"COULD TWO DAYS LIVE AGAIN OF THAT DEAD YEAR."

THERE were necessary delays which postponed the marriage till the end of the coming Easter week, and the panic caused by tolling bells and torchlight funerals having passed away, Gerard was less impatient, willing indeed that events should follow a natural course. Yet although the fever of impatience had spent itself, there was no looking backward, no remorseful thought of her whose character would be blasted for ever by this act of his, or of the unborn child whose future he might have shielded from the chances of evil. Not once did he contemplate the possibility of obtaining his release from Edith Champion, by a full confession of that other tie which to her womanly feeling would have been an

insuperable bar to their marriage. All finer
scruples, all the instincts of honour and of pity
were lost in that tremendous self-love which,
seeing life shrinking to narrowest limits, was
intent on one thing only, to make the most of
the life that remained to him, the life which
was all.

He rallied considerably after that day at
Fiesole, and was equal to being taken about
from church to church by Edith and her eager
cousin, who could not have enough of the Florentine churches in this sacred season. He met
them at the great door of the cathedral on Good
Friday, after they had satisfied their scruples as
pious Anglicans by attending a service at the
English church—service which Rosa denounced
as hatefully low—and he went with them to hear
a litany at the altar under Brunelleschi's dome,
a solemn and awe-inspiring function, a double
semi-circle of priests and choristers within the
marble dado and glass screen that enclosed the
altar—lugubrious chanting unrelieved by the
organ—and at the close of the service a sudden
startling clangour.

Then the doors open, and priests and acolytes

pour out in swift succession, priests in rich vestments, violet and gold, scarlet tippets, white fur, black stoles, a motley train, vanishing quickly towards the sacristy.

And now the crowd troop into the sanctuary, and ascend the steps of the altar, Gerard and his companions following, he curious only, they deeply impressed by that old-world ceremonial. And one by one devout worshippers bend to kiss the jasper slab of the altar, on which stands a golden cross, richly jewelled, which contains a fragment of that cross whereon the Man of Sorrows died for sinful, sorrowing man.

"I hope it was not wrong of me to do as the others did," said Edith presently, as they left the cathedral, her eyes still dim with tears.

"Wrong!" ejaculated Rosa, who had performed the Romanistic rite with unction. "No, indeed. I look forward to the day when we shall have relics in our own churches."

On Holy Saturday there was the spectacular display in front of the cathedral, and at this Gerard was constrained to assist, and to sit in a sunlit window for nearly an hour, watching the humours of the good-tempered crowd in the

Piazza, while the great black tabernacle, covered
with artificial roses, squibs, and Catherine wheels,
awaited the sacred flame which was to set all its
fireworks exploding—flame which descended in
a lightning flash on the wings of a dove from the
lamp on the altar within the cathedral, sacred
light which a pious pilgrim had carried unextin-
guished from the temple in Jerusalem to this
Tuscan city. The dove came rushing down the
invisible guiding wire at the first stroke of noon,
and then with much talk and laughter the crowd
melted out of the Piazza, and the daily traffic
was resumed, and Mrs. Champion's landau came
to the door of the umbrella shop over which she
had hired her window, and they drove away to
the Via Tornabuoni, and the house of Doney,
where luncheon had been ordered and a room
engaged for them, luncheon at which Mrs. Champion's powdered slave officiated, and got in the
way of the brisk waiters, to whom his slow and
solemn movements were an abomination. Only
out of England could there come such sad and
solemn bearing, thought the waiters.

On Sunday there was High Mass at the Church
of S. Maria Annunziata, and Gerard and the two

ladies had seats under the dome, where Mozart's Twelfth Mass was nobly sung by the best choir in Florence, and where priests in vestments of gold and silver, flashing with jewels, gorgeous with embroidery, officiated at the high altar; priests whose splendid raiment suggested the Priesthood of Egypt, in the days when Egyptian splendour was the crowning magnificence of the earth, to be imitated by younger nations, but never to be surpassed.

The music and the splendour, the strain on eye and ear wearied Gerard Hillersdon. He gave a sigh of relief as he took his seat in the laudau opposite Edith and Mrs. Gresham, who regaled them with her raptures about the choir, the voices —that exquisite treble—that magnificent bass. She descanted on every number in the Mass, being one of those persons who wear every subject to tatters.

"And now I think we have had enough of churches," said Gerard, "and we may spend the rest of our lives in the sunshine till we sail away to the Greek Archipelago."

"And till I go back to Suffolk," sighed Mrs. Gresham. "I shall be very glad to see my dear

good man again ; but, oh, how dismal Sandyholme
will be after Florence. And you two happy
creatures will be sailing from island to island,
and your life will be one delicious dream of
summer. Well, I can never be grateful enough
to you, Edith, for having let me see Italy.
Robert Browning said that if his heart were cut
open Italy would be found written upon it; and
so I'm sure it would upon mine, if any one
thought such an insignificant person's heart
worth looking at. And Florence, dear Florence !"

"And the Via Tornabuoni where all the
fashionable shops are—and Doney's, and the
English tea-parties, and the English Church. I
think these things would be found to hold the
highest rank in your Florentine heart, Mrs.
Gresham, though they don't belong to the
Florence of the Medici," said Gerard, glad to
damp middle-aged enthusiasm.

"That shows how very little you understand
my character, Mr. Hillersdon. As for the shops
—they are very smart and artistic, but I would
give all the shops in the Via Tornabuoni for
Whiteley's. I adore Florence most of all for her
historical associations. To think that Catherine

de Medici was reigning Duchess in that noble Palazzo Vecchio—who were the Vecchios, by the by?—some older family I suppose—and that Dante died here, and that Giordino Bruno was burnt here, and Rossini lived here, and Browning! Such a flood of delightful memories," concluded Rosa with a sigh.

The preparations for the wedding hung fire somehow. The day was again postponed. Mrs. Champion had discovered that it would be impossible for her to marry without an interview with her solicitor, and that gentleman had telegraphed his inability to arrive in Florence before the end of the following week.

" He is my trustee," she explained to Gerard, " and I am so unbusiness-like myself that I am peculiarly dependent upon him. I know that I am rich, and that my income is derived from things in the City, railways and foreign loans, don't you know. I write cheques for whatever I want, and Mr. Maddickson has never accused me of being extravagant, so I have no doubt I am very well off. But if I were to marry you without his arranging my affairs I don't know what entanglement might happen."

"What entanglement could there be? Am I not rich enough to live without touching your fortune?"

"My dear Gerard, I didn't mean any doubt of you—not for one moment—but the more money we have the more necessary it must be to arrange things legally, must it not."

"I don't think so. To my mind we are as free as the birds of the air, and all these delays wound me."

"Don't say that, Gerard. You know how firmly I made up my mind not to marry for a year after poor James' death; and if I give way upon that point to gratify a whim of yours——"

"A whim! How lightly you speak. Perhaps you would rather we never married at all."

He was white with anger. She reddened and averted her face.

"Is it so?" he asked.

"No, no, of course not," she answered, "only I don't want to be hustled into marriage."

"Hustled, no, but life is short. If you can't make up your mind to marry me within a fort-night from this day, we will cry quits for my three years' slavery, and will bid each other good-bye. There is a woman in England who won't set up imaginary impediments if I ask her to be my wife."

His voice broke in a suppressed sob as he spoke the last words. Ah, that woman in England, that woman for whom love had been more than honour, that woman who was to be the mother of his child.

"How cruel you are, Gerard," exclaimed Edith, scared at the thought of losing him, "no doubt there are hundreds of women in England who would like to marry you, with your wealth, just as there are hundreds of men who would pretend to be passionately in love with me, for the same motive. We can be married within a fortnight, I have no doubt. I'll telegraph again to Mr. Maddickson, and tell him he must come. I am having my wedding-gown made. You would not like me to be married in black."

"I don't know that I should care. I want to make an end of senseless delays. The *Jersey Lily* is at Spezia, ready for us. Jermyn is to be here this afternoon."

"Jermyn? How strange that you should be so fond of that uncanny personage."

"I never said I was fond of him. He amuses me, that's all. As for his uncanniness, that's a mere fashion. I believe he has left off reading fate in faces. He is too clever to ride any hobby to death."

"And he really got nothing for his fate-reading?"

"He got into society. I think that was all he wanted."

"Bring him to dinner this evening, and he can tell our fortunes again, if he likes."

"Not for me. I prefer a happy ignorance."

Justin Jermyn brought a considerable relief to that party of three which had begun to feel the shadow of an overpowering ennui, Edith ashamed to be sentimental in Rosa Gresham's presence, Rosa infinitely bored, and boring the other two. Mrs. Champion had shrunk from inviting her Florentine friends to meet her betrothed. He looked so wretchedly ill, his humours were so fitful and capricious, that she felt in somewise ashamed of her choice. She could not tell these people how handsome, how brilliant, how charming he had been two or three years ago. She could not inform the world that this intended marriage was the outcome of a girlish romance. She preferred to keep her little Florentine world in complete ignorance of the approaching event. It would be time enough for them to know when she and Gerard were wafted far away on the white wings of the *Jersey Lily*. And later, when he should have recovered his health and good looks, and easy equable manners, later when he and she had become leading lights in London society, she would be proud of him and of their romantic union.

When he recovered his health? There were moments in which she asked herself shudderingly, would that ever be? He pretended to be confident about himself. He told her that to live he needed only happiness and a balmy climate; but she knew that it was a feature of that fatal malady for the patient to be hopeful in the very teeth of despair; and she had seen many indications that had filled her with alarm.

"How I wish you would consult Dr. Wilson," she said one day, when he sank breathless on the marble bench by the fountain, after ten minutes' quiet walking. "He has immense experience in

—in—all chest complaints. I am sure he would be of use to you."

" I have my own doctor in London," Gerard answered curtly. " Your Florentine doctor cannot tell me anything about myself that I don't know; and as for treatment, my valet knows what to do for me. I shall be well when we get further south. Your Florence is as treacherous as her Medicis. The winds from the Apennines are laden with evil.

Jermyn, under existing circumstances, was a decided acquisition. His familiarity with Florence astonished and charmed the two ladies. He knew every church, every palace, every picture, the traditions of every great family that had helped to make the history of the city. Knowledge like this makes every stone eloquent. He was asked to join in all their saunterings and in all their drives, and his presence gave an air of freshness to the simplest pleasures—to the afternoon tea in the garden, and to the long evenings in the salon, when Mrs. Gresham played Chopin and Schubert to her heart's content, while the other three sat afar off and talked.

" My cousin is better than an orchestrion," said

Mrs. Champion, "one has only to turn the handle and she will discourse excellent music the whole evening, and forgive us for not listening to her."

"Yes, but I know that in her inmost heart Mrs. Gresham is pitying us for having a sense wanting," said Jermyn, and then went on with his talk, caring no more for the most delicate rendering of a Rubinstein reverie, than if it had been a hurdy-gurdy grinding a tuneless polka in the road beyond the garden.

    *   *   *   *   *

They all went to Spezia to look at the yacht, a railroad journey of some hours, through a hot arid country, which tried Gerard severely, and bored the other three.

"Who would care to live at Pisa?" said Jermyn, while the train was stopping in the station outside that ancient city. "After one had looked at the Cathedral and Baptistry, the leaning tower and the Campo Santo one would feel that life was done. There is nothing more. And it is a misfortune for everybody but the Cook's tourist that the four things are close together. One can't even pretend to take a long time in seeing them."

Mrs. Champion professed herself delighted with

the yacht. She explored every cabin and corner.
There was a French *chef* engaged, and an Italian
butler, everything was ready for a tour in the
Mediterranean, and the Mediterranean as seen
to-day in this sunlit harbour of Spezia, seemed
a sea that could do no wrong. Jermyn showed
Mrs. Champion her boudoir-dressing-room, with
its ingenious receptacles for her gowns and other
finery, and the cabin for her maid—an infinitesimal
cabin, but full of comforts. He showed her the
grand piano, the electric lamps, all the luxuries
of modern yachting. There was to be no rough-
ing it on board the *Jersey Lily*. The arrangements of this three-hundred-ton yacht left nothing
to be regretted after the most perfect of continental hotels.

Edith was enchanted with everything; but
even in the midst of her enthusiasm a chilling
fear came over her at the thought of Gerard lying
ill in that luxurious cabin, with its silken curtains
and satin pillows, its white and gold Worcester,
in which porcelain was made to imitate carved
ivory. Sickness there—death there—in that
narrow space tricked out for the Loves and
Graces—disease, with its loathly details, playing

havoc with all the beauty of life, illness tending inevitably towards death. She turned from that costly prettiness with a vague horror.

"Don't you like the style?" asked Jermyn, quick to see that revulsion of feeling.

"No; it is much too fine. I think a yacht should be simpler. One does not want the colouring of the Arabian nights on the sea. Picture this cabin in a tempest—all this ornamentation tossed and flying about—a tawdry chaos."

She glanced at Gerard, who stood by, unconcerned in the discussion, obviously caring very little whether she were pleased or not, looking with dull indifferent eye upon the arrangements which had been made for his wedding tour. He had these occasional lapses of abstraction, in which he seemed to drift out of the common life of those around him ; moods of sullen melancholy, which made Edith Champion shiver.

They lunched on board the *Jersey Lily*, and the luncheon was gay enough, but Jermyn and Mrs. Gresham were the chief talkers, and it was Jermyn's laughter that gave an air of joyousness to the meal. Gerard was dreamy and silent; Edith was anxiously watchful of his moods. He was to be her husband soon, and these moods of his would make the colouring of her life. Could she be happy if the mental atmosphere were always dull and dreary? The sapphire blue of the bay, the afternoon light on the Carrara Mountains grew dim and cold in the gloom of her lover's temper; he who long ago, in the days of his poverty, had been so joyous a spirit.

She thought of James Champion, and of those monotonous visits to the house at Finchley, the weary hours she had spent trying to make conversation for a sick man, weighed down by the sense of his own infirmities, unable to take pleasure in anything. "Would Gerard ever be like that?" she asked herself with an aching dread; would he, too, die as Champion had died, "first a'top." She looked at his sunken cheek and hollow eye; she noted his absent manner; and she felt no assurance of exemption from that dreadful doom.

Happily, however, the dark mood did not last long, and Gerard was full of animation during the return journey, full of talk about the intended cruise of the *Jersey Lily*. He had talked it all over with the sailing master. They had looked at charts, they had discussed the ports they were to touch—the islands which were worth stopping at—so many days for Cyprus, and so many for Corfu. They were to spend part of the autumn in Palestine, and to winter in Egypt, and then come slowly back to Naples in the early spring, and from Naples follow the coast in a leisurely way to Nice, and then good-bye, *Jersey Lily*, and as fast as the *Rapide* can carry us homeward, to London and Hillersdon House, and all the glories of a London season. The prospect sounded delightful, discussed in one of Gerard's brightest moods, as they travelled from Pisa to Florence; but the outlook was not quite so joyous half-an-hour later when a laugh at one of Jermyn's cynical flashes brought on a violent fit of coughing, one of those exhausting, suffocating paroxysms which had moved the fair Bavarian to such deep pity.

CHAPTER V.

"AND ALL SHALL PASSE, AND THUS TAKE I MY
LEAVE."

MR. MADDICKSON, Mrs. Champion's solicitor and
trustee, arrived early in the following week—
three days sooner than he had declared possible,
urged to this haste by importunate telegrams.
He was bidden to a dinner at which Mr. Hillersdon
and his friend Jermyn were the only guests, in
order that everything might be discussed that
needed discussion, and that the lady's confidential
adviser might make the acquaintance of her
future husband.

It was a delicious evening, balmier than many
an English July. The Easter moon had waned,
and the slender crescent of the new moon shone
silvery pale in a rose-flushed heaven, a heaven
where in that lovely after-glow the first stars

glimmered faint and wan. Mrs. Champion was in the garden with Gerard and Jermyn when the lawyer arrived, spruce and prim in his impeccable evening dress, a man who deemed it a duty he owed to his profession to employ only the most admirable of tailors. The two young men were lounging on garden-chairs in the circle by the fountain, beyond which the great pink peonies made a background of bloom and verdure. Mr. Maddickson's short-sighted eyes took the big pink blossoms for gigantic roses, such as a man might expect to find in Italy. He looked from one of the young men to the other, and at once made up his mind that the lady's *fiancé* was the fair youth leaning against the fountain, his head thrown back a little and the rosy light upon his face as he looked up at Mrs. Gresham, whose speech had just moved him to joyous laughter. Quite the sort of young man to catch a widow's fancy, thought Mr. Maddickson, who supposed it was in the nature of widows to be frivolous.

He felt a cold shiver—happily only perceptible to himself—when Mrs. Champion introduced the pale hollow-eyed young man, with slightly bent shoulders and an unmistakable air of decay, as

Mr. Hillersdon. He lost his usual aplomb, and was awkwardly silent for some minutes after that introduction.

There was a brief discussion between the lovers and the lawyer late in the evening, while Rosa and Mr. Jermyn were in the loggia, he smoking, she declaring she adored the odour of tobacco.

There were no difficulties, Mr. Maddickson told his client and her betrothed, and the settlements might be of the simplest form. He proposed as a matter of course that the lady's fortune should be settled on herself and her children, giving her full disposing power if there should be no children.

"You are so rich, Mr. Hillersdon," said the lawyer, "that these details can hardly interest you."

"They don't. I wanted Mrs. Champion to marry me out of hand ten days ago, without any legal fussification or delay. I thought the Married Women's Property Act would protect her estate, even in the event of my squandering my fortune, which I am hardly likely to do."

" It is always best to have these matters quietly

discussed," said Mr. Maddickson. "A hasty marriage is rarely a wise marriage."

He gave a little sigh as he uttered this tolerably safe opinion, and rose to take leave ; but before departing he paused to address Mrs. Champion in a lower tone.

"I should much like to have a little talk with you to-morrow," he said. "Shall I find you at home if I call ?"

"Not in the afternoon. We are to drive to the Certosa."

"In the morning, then? I can be here at any hour you like."

"Come at twelve, and stay to lunch. We lunch at half-past twelve." And then, going with him towards the door of the salon, she said in a lower tone, "I conclude there is really nothing now to hinder my marriage ?"

"Nothing, except your own inclination. I think you are marrying too soon; but we will talk of that to-morrow."

When he was gone she had an uncomfortable feeling that he would have something disagreeable to say to her when he came in the morning. People who ask for interviews in that elaborately urgent manner are seldom the bearers of pleasant tidings. She had a sleepless night, agitated by vague dread.

Mr. Maddickson was punctual to a minute, for the timepiece in the salon chimed the hour as the footman announced him, looking as fresh and trim in his checked travelling suit as he had looked in evening dress; clean-shaved, the image of respectability not unconscious of the latest fashion.

"I have spent the morning at the Academy," he said blandly, "and have become a convert to the Early Italian school. I don't wonder at Hunt, and Millais, and those young fellows, now I have seen those two walls—one splendid with the exquisite finish and lustrous colour of Giotto, Boticelli, Filippo Lippi, Fra Angelico and their disciples, and the other covered with a collection of gloomy daubs, in the high classical manner, by the worst painters of the school that came after Raffaelle."

"You have something serious to say to me?" said Edith, not caring a jot for Mr. Maddickson's opinions on art.

"Something very serious."

" Then pray come at once to the point, or my cousin will have returned from her walk before you have finished."

" My dear Mrs. Champion, I have not had the pleasure of much social intercourse with you, but I have been interested in you professionally ever since your marriage, and my position as your trustee should give me some of the privileges of friendship."

" Consider that you have every privilege that friendship can give," she exclaimed impatiently ; " but pray don't beat about the bush."

" Are you seriously attached to Mr. Hillersdon ? "

" Of course I am, or I should not be thinking of marrying him within a year of my husband's death. We were boy and girl sweethearts, and I would have married him without a penny if it hadn't been for my people. They insisted upon my marrying Mr. Champion, and he was very good to me, and I was very happy with him ; but the old love was never forgotten, and now that I am free what can be more natural than that I should marry my first love ? "

" What indeed, but for one unhappy fact."

" What is that, pray ? "

" You have engaged yourself to a dying man. Surely, my dear friend, you must see that this poor young man has the stamp of death upon him."

" I know that he is out of health. He spent the winter in England, which he ought not to have done. We are going on a long cruise; we shall be in a climate that will cure him. He has been neglectful of his health, and has had no one to take care of him. It will be all different when we are married."

" My dear Mrs. Champion, don't deceive yourself," the lawyer said earnestly. " You don't pretend to have the power of working miracles, I suppose; and the raising of Lazarus was hardly a greater miracle than this young man's restoration to health would be. I tell you—for it is my duty to tell you—that he is dying. I have seen such cases before—cases of atrophy, heart and lungs both attacked, a gradual extinction of life. Doctor him as you may, nurse him as you may, this young man must die. Marry him if you like—I shall deeply regret it if you do—and be sure you will be again a widow before the year is out."

Tears were streaming down Mrs. Champion's cheeks. This matter-of-fact, hard-headed lawyer had only put into plain words the dim forebodings, the indistinct terrors which had been weighing her down since Gerard came to Florence. The change she had seen in him on his first coming had frozen her heart; and not once in all the hours they had spent together had he seemed the same man she had loved a year ago. Between them there was a shadow, indescribable, indefinable, which she now knew for the shadow of death.

Mr. Maddickson made no ill-advised attempt at consolation. He knew that in such a case there must be tears, and he let her cry, waiting deferentially for anything she might have to say.

"I had such a sad time with Mr. Champion," she said presently. "It was so painful to see his mind gradually going. You know what a long, long illness it was, nearly a year. I was a great deal with him. I wanted him to feel that he was never abandoned. It was my duty —but it was a sad trial. It left me an old woman."

This was a mere *façon de parler*, since Mrs.
Champion's sufferings during her husband's illness had not written a line upon her brow or
silvered a single hair.

"It was a dreadful time," she sighed, after a
pause. "I don't think I could go through it
again."

"It would be very hard if you were called
upon to do so," said Mr. Maddickson; and Mrs.
Champion felt that it would be hard.

She wanted the joys of life; not to be steeped
to the lips in the apprehensions and agonies of
fast-approaching death.

"Does he really seem to you so very ill?" she
asked presently.

"Nobody can doubt it who looks in his face.
He has some medical attendant in Florence, I
suppose."

"No. I wanted him to see Dr. Wilson, but he
refused. He says that he knows all about himself, that he has nothing to learn from any
doctor."

"And is he hopeful about himself?"

"Yes, fairly hopeful, I think."

"Poor fellow. I am sorry for him; but I

should be sorrier for you if you were foolish enough to marry him."

Mrs. Gresham came in from her morning walk, loquacious and gushing as usual. She had been up the hill, and had taken another look at that noble David, and at the view of Florence from the terrace.

"Florence is in one of her too delicious moods," she said, "all sunlight and colour. My heart aches at the thought of going away, but the place will live in my memory for the rest of my life. I shall often be thinking of San Miniato on that hill of gardens, and the after-noon light stealing in through the transparent marble in the apse, when I am sitting in our own dear old grey church."

Gerard and his friend appeared before Rosa had left off talking, and there was an immediate adjournment to luncheon, at which meal conver-sation was chiefly sustained by Mr. Maddickson and Mr. Jermyn, with a running accompaniment by Rosa, who broke in at every point of the argument upon Italian art to express opinions which were as irrelevant as they were enthusiastic.

Edith Champion was silent and thoughtful all through luncheon, and more than usually observant of her lover, who looked tired and depressed, scarcely ate anything, and drank only a single glass of claret. Seeing this, she proposed a postponement of the drive to the Carthusian monastery. The afternoon was warm to sultriness, the road would be dusty, and the going up and down steps would tire Gerard. He was altogether indifferent, would go or not go as she pleased; whereupon she settled that Mr. Jermyn and Mr. Maddickson should drive with Mrs. Gresham, who was greedy of sight-seeing, and always anxious to repeat expeditions, while Gerard and his *fiancée* could spend their after-noon in the garden.

That afternoon in the garden hung somewhat heavily on the engaged lovers. They had spent a good many afternoons and evenings together since Gerard's arrival in Florence, afternoons and evenings that had been virtually *tête-à-tête*, in-asmuch as Rosa was very discreet, and preferred her piano to the society of the lovers. Thus they had talked of the past and of the future— their plans, their houses, their views of society, till there was no fresh ground left to travel over. Edith could talk only of actualities. The dim labyrinth of metaphysical speculations, the dreamland of poets were worlds that were closed against her essentially earthly intellect. Gerard had never so felt the something wanting in her mind as he felt it now that he had known the companionship of Hester's more spiritual nature. With Hester he had never been at a loss for subjects of conversation, even in the monotony of their isolated lives.

The fountain, with its border of aram lilies, the pink peonies, the blood-red cups of tulips that filled a border on a lower terrace, the perfume of lilac and hawthorn, were all a weariness to him, as he sat upon the marble bench, and watched the water leaping towards the sunlight, only to fall and break in rainbow-coloured spray —symbolic of the mind of man, always aspiring, never attaining. He was in one of those listless moods when every nerve seems relaxed, every sense dulled. Moods in which a man cares for nothing, hopes for nothing, and, save for the dread of death, would willingly have done with life. Was it so vast a boon, after all, he asked

himself, this life to which he clung so passionately? No boon, perhaps, but it was all.
There was the rub. After this nothing. He
might sicken of the loveliness around him, of
the glory of colour and the endless variety of
light, of the distant view of the mountains,
where the snow yet lingered. These might
pall, but who would willingly exchange these
for darkness and dust, and the world's for-
getfulness?

In the discussion on the previous evening it
had been settled that the wedding was to take
place on the coming Saturday. Mr. Maddickson
had tried his utmost, by various suggestions,
to defer the date, but Gerard had been inflexible,
and had carried his point. In three days these
two who sat listless and silent in the afternoon
sunlight, she sheltered by a large white parasol,
he baring his head to the warmth, were to be
man and wife. There was nothing more for
them to talk about. Their future was decided.

Gerard did not wait for the return of the
party from the Certosa, or for afternoon tea.
He pleaded letters that must be written for
the evening post, and left before five o'clock,

promising to dine at the villa as usual. Edith
walked with him to the gate, and kissed him
affectionately at parting, detaining him a little
at the last, as if she were loth to let him leave
her. And then, when his carriage wheels were
out of hearing she went slowly back to the house,
with streaming eyes, went straight to her room,
and flung herself upon a sofa, and sobbed as if
her heart would break. She was so sorry for him.
She mourned him as one already dead. She
mourned for her old love, which had died with
the man she had loved, the light-hearted lover
of five years ago. It was hard to acknowledge,
it was bitter to bear, but she knew that Mr.
Maddickson was right, and that to marry Gerard
Hillersdon was only to take upon herself the
burden of an inevitable sorrow.

"If I believed that I could make his last days
happy, I would gladly marry him," she told
herself. "I would think nothing of myself or
of my own sorrow afterwards, my second widowhood; but I have seen enough of him now to
know that I can't make him happy. He is no
happier with me than he is anywhere else. He
is only bored and wearied. I am nothing to him,

and his wish to marry me can only be the desire
to keep his promise. I believe it will be a relief
to his mind if I release him from that promise.
It was wrong of me to exact such a vow; very,
very wrong."

She remembered that day in Hertford Street,
when she had urged him to be true to her, when
she had said to him of his promise—"It is an
oath!" Ah, how passionately she had loved
him in those days, how impossible happiness
had seemed to her without him. She had
thought that if he were to marry any other
woman she would die. There would be no help
for her, nothing left. Wealth, and all that it
can buy, independence, beauty, youth, would be
worthless without him. And now she was
meditating with what words, with what gentle
circumlocution she should free herself from a
tie that had become terrible to her, the bond
between the living and the dead. Mr. Maddickson's warning had suggested no new idea; the
mournful conviction had been growing in her
mind ever since Gerard came to Florence. She
knew that he was doomed, and that the day of
doom could not be far off.

Gerard wrote his letters—to his mother, telling her of the intended wedding, to his banker, to his lawyer—and then threw himself down to rest upon a sofa. He slept more than an hour, and was only awakened by some one coming into the room. It was Jermyn, who approached him with an open letter in his hand.

"Have you come straight from the Certosa, or did you stop to tea at the villa?" Gerard asked, and then seeing the altered light, "Is it time to dress for dinner?"

"I don't think you will care about dining in Florence to-night. I have some bad news for you," replied Jermyn gravely, looking down at the letter.

"Bad news—you have bad news—for me. From Helmsleigh—no, from Lowcombe?"

"Yes, it is from Lowcombe. It comes by a side wind, in a letter from Matt Muller."

"Give me the letter," cried Gerard, ghastly pale, snatching it from Jermyn's hand.

He was too agitated for the first few moments to see the portion of the letter which referred to his own evil fortune. He saw only words about the house Muller was building—abuse of architect and builder—the mistakes of one, the dilatoriness of the other. It was only when Jermyn put a hand over his shoulder and pointed to the bottom of a closely written page that he saw where the bad news began.

"You are interested I know in that pretty young woman at the Rosary, though I could never persuade you to introduce me to her. You will be sorry to hear that she is in sad trouble, poor girl, trouble which is all the sadder because the man who called himself her husband seems to have deserted her. There was a baby born at the Rosary—a baby that came upon this mortal scene before he was expected, poor little beggar. The old father's sudden death, I believe, was the cause of this premature event—and ten days or a fortnight after the baby's birth the young mother went clean off her head, and only last night she escaped from the two nurses who had care of her, and wandered away by the river, with, I believe, the intention of drowning herself. The baby was drowned, and the mother only escaped by the happy chance of a couple of Cockneys who were rowing down from Oxford, one of whom swam to the poor girl's rescue very pluckily. There is to be an inquest on the infant this afternoon, and I don't know in whose custody the mother now is, but I suppose some one is looking after her. My builder's foreman lives at Lowcombe, and he tells me there has been a great deal of excitement about the affair, for this Mr. Hanley is supposed to be a man of large means, and he is thought to have acted cruelly to this poor young woman, wife or no wife, in leaving her at such a time."

"Cruelly," muttered Gerard, "yes, with the cruelty of devils. But she would not come with me—it was her choice to stay. How could I tell? Is it true, Jermyn? Is this some trick of yours to frighten me?"

"It is no trick. I thought it best to show you the letter, that you should know the worst at once."

"The worst, yes. Hester, perhaps, a prisoner —accused of murdering her child! The worst! Oh, what a wretch I have been. When can I get away from here? How soon can I get to London?"

"You can leave Florence to-night; I will

go with you. The Mont Cenis, I think, is the quickest way. I'll arrange everything with your servant. Shall you see Mrs. Champion before you go?"

"See her, no. What good would that do?"

"We were to have dined with her this evening. Shall I write an apology in your name?"

"Yes, you can do that. Tell her I am called away upon a matter of life and death; that I don't know how long it may be before I can return to Florence. You may make my apology as abject as you like. I doubt if she and I will ever meet again."

"You are agitating yourself too much, Hillersdon," remonstrated Jermyn.

"Can there be too much in the matter? Can anything be too much? Oh, how nobly that girl loved me—how generous, how uncomplaining she was! And I have murdered her! First I slew her good name, and now her child is murdered—murdered by me, not by her, and she has to bear the brand of infamy, as if she were a common felon."

"She will not be considered guilty. It will be

known that she was irresponsible. People will be good to her, be sure of that."

"Will the law be good to her? The law which takes no account of circumstances, the law which settles everything by hard and fast lines. To-morrow! It will be the day after to-morrow before we are at Lowcombe, travel how we may. What ages to wait. Get me some telegraph forms. I'll telegraph to the Rector. He is a good man, and may be able to help us."

"To help *us*," he said, making himself one with Hester in her trouble, re-united to her by calamity. He forgot in his agony how false he had been to her, forgot that he had planned to spend the rest of his days far away from her. The thought of her sorrow made her newly dear to him.

He made his appeal to the Rector in the most urgent form that occurred to him. He implored that good man for Christian charity to be kind to the ill-used girl whom he knew as Mrs. Hanley. He urged him to spare no outlay in providing legal help, if legal help were needed. If she was able to understand anything she was

to be assured that her husband would be with
her without the loss of an hour.

He used that word husband, careless of consequences, albeit in three days he was to have
become the husband of another woman.

While he wrote the telegram Jermyn looked
at the time-table. The train for Turin left in an
hour. The order was given to the valet, everything was to be ready, and a fly was to be at
the door in three-quarters of an hour.

"You'll have some dinner served here, I
suppose," suggested Jermyn.

"Do you think I can eat at such a time?"

"Well, no, perhaps not. You've been hard
hit; but it would be better if you could fortify
yourself for a long journey."

"Take care of yourself," answered Gerard,
curtly.

"Thanks. I always do that," said Jermyn.
"I'll go down to the *table d'hôte* when I've written
to Mrs. Champion."

He seated himself to write, but before he began
a waiter brought in a letter for Mr. Hillersdon.
Gerard knew the hand, the thick vellum paper
with its narrow black border and massive black

monogram; he knew the delicate perfume which
always accompanied such letters, a faint suggestion of violets or lilies.

The letter was brief:—

"DEAR GERARD,

"I have a wretched headache, and
am altogether depressed and miserable this
evening, so I must ask you and your friend
to postpone your visit. I am not fit company
for any one. I will write again to-morrow. I
have much to say to you—that must be said
somehow. It may be easier to write than to
speak.—Ever yours.

"EDITH."

A curious letter to be written by a woman
from whom he had parted only a few hours
earlier. What could she have to say to him
that could not have been said by the fountain
when they two sat silent, as if spellbound in
the languid air? He wondered at the wording
of her letter, but with faintest interest in the
question. Everything that affected his life at
Florence had grown dim and blurred, like a

faded photograph. The image of Edith Champion had receded into the background of his
thoughts.

"Here is a letter that will save you the trouble
of an elaborate apology," he said to Jermyn, "a
letter which I can answer myself."

He scrawled a hurried line announcing his departure from Florence.

"You have deferred our wedding day twice,"
he wrote. "Fate constrains me to defer it for the
third time. I will write to you from London."

CHAPTER VI.

"FROM THE WARM WILD KISS TO THE COLD."

GERARD travelled as fast as trains and boat would take him, but it was noon on the second day after he had left Florence before he arrived at the nearest station to Lowcombe, with the prospect of over an hour's drive behind an indifferent horse before he could reach the Rosary and know the worst. He was alone. He had sent his valet to Hillersdon House, and had resolutely refused Jermyn's company, although Jermyn had urged that he was hardly in a state of health to risk a solitary journey, or the consequences of further ill news.

"If there is anything worse to be told, you could not help me to bear the blow," Gerard answered gloomily. "Nor would she care to see you with me. You were no favourite of

hers; and perhaps if it had not been for you
I should never have left her."

They had searched all the morning papers
they could obtain during the journey from
Dover to Charing Cross, to discover any paragraph that might record the calamity at
Lowcombe—for any report of the inquest on
the infant, or the rescue of the mother. It
was at least some relief to find no such record.
Whatever had happened, the report had, by
happy chance or kindly influence, been kept
out of the papers. Hester's name and Hester's
sorrows were not bandied about in a social
leader, or even made the subject of a paragraph.

Gerard reached Lowcombe, therefore, in absolute ignorance of anything that might have
happened since Mr. Muller's letter was written.
He drove straight to the Rosary, where garden
and shrubberies looked dull and dreary under
a sunless sky. It seemed as if he had left
summer on the other side of the Alps—as if
he had come into a land where there was no
summer, only a neutral season, which meant
gloom and smoke in London, and dim greyness
in the country.

His heart grew cold at sight of the windows. The blinds were down. The house was either uninhabited, or inhabited by Death.

He rang violently, and rang again, but had to wait nearly five minutes, an interval of torturing suspense, before a housemaid opened the door, her countenance only just composing itself after the broad grin that had rewarded the baker's last sally. The baker's cart rattled away from the back door while the housemaid stood at the front door answering her master's eager questions.

" Where is your mistress ? She—she is not—— "

He could not utter the word that would have given shape to his fear. Happily the girl was sympathetic, although frivolous-minded as to bakers and butcher-boys. She did not prolong his agony.

" She is not any worse, sir. She's very bad, but not worse."

" Can I see her at once—would it do her any harm to see me ? " he asked, going towards the staircase.

" She's not here, sir. She's at the Rectory.

Mr. Gilstone had her taken there after she was saved from drowning by those two London gentlemen. She was took to the Rose and Crown, as that was the nearest house to the river; the two gentlemen carried her there, quite unconscious, and they had hard work to bring her round. And they sent here for the two nurses, and they kep' her there, at the Rose, till next morning; and then the Rector he had her taken to the Rectory, and his sister is helping to nurse her."

"They are good souls," cried Gerard, "true Christians. What shall we do in our troubles when there are no more Christians in the world?" he thought, deeply touched by kindness from the man whose sympathy he had repulsed.

"Is your mistress dangerously ill?" he asked.

"She has been in great danger, sir; and I don't think she's out of danger yet. I was at the Rectory last night to inquire, and one of the nurses told me it was a very critical case. But she's well nursed, and well cared for, sir. You can make yourself happy about that."

"Happy! I can never know happiness again!"

"Oh, yes, but you will, sir, when Mrs. Hanley gets well. I make no doubt they'll pull her through."

"And her baby——"

"Oh, the poor little thing! He was such a weakly little mite—I'm sure he's better off in Heaven; if his poor mother could only think so, when she comes round and has to be told about it."

"There was an inquest, wasn't there?"

"Well, yes, sir, there was an inquest at the Rose and Crown; but it wasn't much of an inquest," Mary Jane added, in a comforting tone. "The baker told me the coroner and the other gentlemen weren't in the room above ten minutes. 'Death by misadventure,' that was the verdict. Everybody was so sorry for the poor young lady. And it was a misadventure, for if the night nurse hadn't left the door unfastened, and fallen asleep in her easy-chair, nothing need have gone wrong. It was all along of her carelessness. My poor young mistress got up and put on her morning gown and slippers, and took the baby out of his bassinette, and went downstairs and out of the drawing-room window, and she must have gone across the lawn down to the towing path, and wandered and wandered for nearly two miles before she threw herself in just by the little backwater where she and you used to be so fond of sitting in the punt, where we used to send your lunch out to you."

"Yes, yes, I know. It was there, was it?"

The thought of the hours they had spent there, hours of blissful tranquillity, steeped in the summer warmth, the golden light, sweet odours of field flowers, soothing ripple of water, and rustle of willow branches. What happy hours of delight in all that is most exquisite in literature, Milton, Keats, Tennyson, Rosetti, in that music of words which is second only to the music of sweet concords and exquisite harmonies. Oh, happy hours, happy days, bliss which he had dreamed might last out all his life, and lengthen life by its reposeful sweetness. And now he had to think of his dear love, the fair Egeria of those peaceful hours, wandering distraught along that river bank, choosing by some dim instinct of the dreaming mind that spot above all other spots in which to seek death and oblivion.

"Tell me how it all happened," he said to the girl. "Mr. Davenport's death—was it very sudden?"

"Dreadfully sudden, sir. It was the shock of her father's death which made my mistress so bad. She was very down-hearted after you went abroad. We could all see that, though none of us ever see her cry. She was too much the lady to give way before servants; but we could tell by her face in the morning that she'd been awake most of the night, and that she'd been crying a good deal. And then she'd pull herself together, as you may say, and be bright and cheerful with the old gentleman, and sit with him, and talk to him, and walk beside his chair, and give all her thoughts and all her time to making him as happy as he could be made. And it wasn't easy work, for after you was gone he took a sort of restless fit, and he was always asking about you, the nurse said, and he seemed uneasy at not seeing you. And he used to talk to poor Mrs. Hanley in a disagreeable way, and he was quite nasty to

her, his man told me, and was always blaming
her, as if she hadn't done her best for him.
He was very cruel to her, I think; but I suppose
it must have been because he was worse in
himself. And one day he was particularly
unkind, and she left him in tears, and went
out into the garden and sat there alone by
the river, and didn't go to her father's room
to sit with him while he took his lunch, as
she generally did, and his man found her sitting
in the garden very low-spirited, when he went
to tell her that he and the nurse were going
to dinner. Missus always used to sit with the
old gentleman while those two had their dinner.
And she went up to his room, and found him
lying quietly on the sofa, and she sat there
over an hour, for those two used to take their
time over their dinner, no doubt thinking he
was asleep all the time, and then, just as the
nurse was going upstairs, we all heard a dreadful
shriek and a fall, and we found her lying in-
sensible on the floor near the sofa, where her
father lay dead. She had gone to him, and
spoken to him, and touched him, and found
him dead."

There was a pause, a silence broken only by Gerard's agonised sobbing, as he sat at the table where he had planned his new novel, in the happy morning of his love, sat with his head bent low upon his folded arms.

" She was very bad all that day and night, and Dr. Mivor telegraphed for a second nurse, for he said we was in for a bad business. She was quite light-headed, poor young lady, and it was heart-breaking to hear her asking for you, and why you didn't go to her, and talking about her father, and begging him to forgive her, as if she had any need of forgiveness, when she'd devoted herself to making him comfortable and happy from the first hour he was took. And three days after his death the poor little baby was born, and she was quite out of her mind all the time and didn't seem to care about the baby, though he was a dear pretty little thing—but very tiny and weak, and I don't think he'd have lived long, even with the best of care. A week after he was born the fever went down a bit, and she seemed to be coming more to herself. There was a great change in her, and she left off talking wildly, and she seemed to understand that her father was dead, and that you were far away; and everybody thought she was better. I suppose this made the night-nurse a little less watchful. Both nurses had been very careful of her while she was so bad with the fever, but they began to take things easier, and to drop asleep in the arm-chair. They'd both had a hard time of it for the first week. And I think that's about all I can tell you, sir; except that Mr. Davenport was buried in Lowcombe churchyard nearly a fortnight ago."

"Thank you for telling me so much. You are a good girl."

"Shall I get you a bit of lunch, sir? You are looking so tired and ill."

"No, thank you, Mary, I shall eat nothing till I get to the Rectory. Good day. Take care of the house, and keep everything in good order till your mistress and I come back. By the way, who has been supplying you with money since your mistress fell ill? Have you had any difficulty in providing for expenses?"

"No, sir; the cook knew where mistress kept her money, and she made bold to unlock the drawer and take out what was wanted. There was a fifty-pound note and some sovereigns in the drawer. There has been plenty to pay the nurses and gardeners, and to provide any ready money that was wanted. Cook has kept an account of everything. The undertaker has not been paid anything, nor the doctor, but they know their money's safe."

The fly was waiting, and it took Gerard to the Rectory with very little loss of time, yet to his agonised mind the distance seemed long, the horse slower than such hirelings usually are. Fate had used him almost better than he had hoped. The coroner's verdict freed Hester from all shadow of blame in the child's death—his child; that child of whose existence he had taken so little thought, deeming that he had done enough when he had left ample funds at the mother's disposal. He had cared but for one thing, to make the best and the most of his own waning days—and the thought of the child that was to be born to him had awakened no tender feeling, only an aching envy of that young fresh life in which doubtless his qualities and characteristics would live again under happier conditions, the life which would be tasting all the sweetest things that this world can give—love, ambition, pride, luxury, the mastery of men— while he was lying cold and dumb, cheated by inexorable Death out of the riches which Fortune had flung into his lap. Fate had given with one hand, and had taken away with the other. No, he had never felt as an expectant father should feel. The thought of his duty to the child had never urged him to repair the wrong he had done the mother—but now remorse weighed heavy on his heart, and he hated himself for the egotism which had governed him in all his relations with the woman he had pretended to love. He had glossed over all that was guilty in their union; he had kissed away her tears, and made light of her remorse; he had compared her to Shelley's Mary, forgetting that Shelley was as eager to legalise his union as the most conforming Christian in the land. He looked back upon the happy days of their love, and knew that when he was happiest Hester's life had been under the shadow of an ever-present regret, knew that while she was generous and devoted he had been selfish and false, soothing her conscience with shallowest sophistries.

Yes, he had used her ill, the woman who loved him; had killed her it might be; or had killed her intellect, leaving her to go down to old age through the long joyous years, a mindless wreck; she who was once so happy, a lovely ethereal creature in whom mind and heart were paramount over clay.

The Rector received him coldly, and with a countenance which unaccustomed anger made strange and forbidding. When a benevolent man is angry his anger has a deeper root and a more chilling aspect than the ready displeasure of less kindly spirits. For Mr. Gilstone to be angry meant a complete upheaval of a nature that was made up of sympathy and compassion. But here for once was a man with whom he could not sympathise, for whom his present feeling was abhorrence.

"Is she recovering? May I see her?" asked Gerard, on the threshold of the Rector's study, chilled by that stern countenance, yet too full of the thought of Hester to delay his questioning.

"She is a shade better this morning," the Rector answered coldly, "but she is far too ill for you to see her—at any rate until the doctor

thinks it safe—and when you are allowed to see
her it is doubtful whether she will recognise you.
She is in a world of her own, poor soul, a world
of shadows."

"Is her mind quite gone?" faltered Gerard.
"Does the doctor fear—— "

"The doctor fears more for her life than for
her mind. If we can save her life the mind may
recover its balance as strength returns. That is
his opinion and mine. I have seen such cases
before—and the result has generally been happy;
but in those cases we had to deal with a ruder
clay. All that is finest in this girl's nature will
tell against her recovery. There is a heavy
account against you here, Mr. Hanley."

"I know, I know," cried Gerard, with his face
turned from the Rector, as he stood looking out
of the window, across the flame-coloured tulips,
the level lawn, towards the churchyard, conscious of nothing which his eyes looked at, only
turning his face away to hide his agony.

"A heavy account; you have brought dis-
honour upon a woman whose every instinct
makes for virtue. You have broken her heart
by your desertion."

"I did not desert her——"

"Not as the world reckons desertion perhaps. You left her a house and servants and a bundle of bank-notes; but you left her just when she had the most need of sympathy—left her to face an ordeal which might mean death—left her under conditions which no man with a heart could have ignored."

"I was inconsiderate—selfish—cruel. Say the worst you can of me. Lash me with bitter words. I acknowledge my iniquity. I was only just recovered from a dangerous illness——"

"Through which she nursed you. I have heard of her devotion."

"Through which she nursed me. I was not ungrateful—but I was wretched, borne down by the knowledge that I had only a short time to live. Ah, Rector, you in your green old age, sturdy, vigorous, with strength to enjoy the fulness of life even now when your hair is silver— you can hardly realise what a young man feels who has unexpectedly inherited a vast fortune, and who while the delight of possession is still fresh and wonderful, is told that his life is narrowed to a few precarious years—that if he is to last out even that short span he must watch himself with jealous care, husband his emotions, lest the natural joys of youth should waste the oil in the lamp. This was what I was told. Be happy, be calm, be tranquil, said my physician; in other words, be self-indulgent, care for nothing and for no one but self. And I felt that yonder house was killing me. The shadow of that old man's decaying age darkened my fading youth. If Hester would have gone with me to the South there would have been no break in our union—at least I think not—though there was another claim——"

" She refused to leave her father ? "

" Yes. She preferred him to me. It was her own free choice."

" Well, there are excuses for you, perhaps; and the result of your conduct has been so disastrous that you need no sermon from me. If you have a heart, the rest of your life must be darkened by remorse. Your child's death lies at your door."

" Does she remember that dreadful night —does she grieve for the child ? " asked Gerard.

"Happily not. I have told you she is living in a world of shadows."

"Let me see her," pleaded Gerard. "You don't know how fondly she loves me—how dear we have been to each other. Her mind will awaken at the sound of my voice."

"Awaken to the memory of all that she has suffered. Would that be an advantage? Mr. Mivor must be the judge as to whether she ought to see you. If he finds no objection—— "

"When will he be here?"

"Not till the evening."

"Then I'll go to his house, and bring him here if necessary. Mr. Gilstone," said Gerard, stopping on the threshold, as the Rector followed him to the hall, "you are a good man. However hardly you may think of me, nothing will ever lessen my gratitude to you—and in the short time I may yet have to live I hope to prove that with me gratitude means something more than a word."

The Rector gave him his hand in silence, and Gerard got into the fly and was driven to Mr. Mivor's comfortable cottage, a low, white-walled building with a thatched roof, at the end of the straggling village street.

Mr. Mivor was surprised to see him, but asked no questions.

"I should have telegraphed to you more than a fortnight ago if I had known where to find you," he said. "I am glad you have come back. Mrs. Hanley is a little better to-day—only a little. We must be thankful for the least improvement, and we must try not to lose ground again."

"She has been dangerously ill, I am told?"

"Dangerously! Yes, I should think so. She has been on the brink of death, not once, but several times since the birth of her child. And since the fever took a bad turn—the night she tried to make away with herself—her condition has been all but hopeless, until yesterday, when there were signs of rallying."

"May I see her?"

"I don't think it could do her any harm. She won't know you."

"Yes, she will! She will know me. She may not recognise people who are almost strangers to her, but she will know me—— "

"Poor lady! She hardly knows herself. Ask her who she is, and she will tell you a strange story. All we can hope is that with returning strength mind and memory will return. I will go to the Rectory with you, and if I find her as tranquil as she was this morning you shall see her."

They were at the Rectory ten minutes later, and this time Mr. Gilstone received Gerard with kindliness. He had given speech to his indignation, and now his natural benevolence pleaded with him for the repentant sinner. He received Gerard in his study, while the doctor went to see his patient.

" You have not asked me why I took upon myself to have Mrs. Hanley brought to this house, rather than to her own," he said.

" I had no need to ask. It was easy for me to understand your kindly motive. You would not let her re-enter a house in which she had tasted such misery—you wished to surround her with fresh objects, in a peaceful shelter where nothing would remind her of her past sufferings."

"That was one motive. The other was to place her under the care of my sister. However devoted hired nurses may be, and I have nothing to say against the woman who is now nursing

Mrs. Hanley, it is well that there should be some one near who is not a hireling, who works for love, and not for wages. My sister's heart has gone out to this poor lady."

Mr. Mivor appeared at the study door, which had been left open while Gerard waited, his ear strained to catch every sound in the quiet, orderly house, where all the machinery of life went on with a calm regularity that knew no change save the changing seasons. The silence of the house oppressed Gerard as he went upstairs, filled with an aching fear. Was he to find her cold and unconscious of his presence— the girl who had hung upon him with despairing love when they parted, less than a month ago?

A door was opened, a woman in a white cap and apron looked at him gravely, and drew aside. It was the nurse who had waited upon old Nicholas Davenport, and even in this moment the association made him shudder. And then, scarcely conscious of his own movements, he was standing in a sunlit room where a young woman in a white morning gown, and with hollow cheeks and soft, fair hair, cropped close to the well-shaped head, was sitting at a table playing with the flowers that were strewn upon it.

" Hester, Hester, my darling, I have come back to you," he cried, in a heart-broken voice, and then he fell on his knees beside her chair, and tried to draw the fair face down towards his quivering lips, but she shrank away from him with a scared look.

In spite of the doctor's warning he was unprepared for this. He had hugged himself with the belief that had her mind wandered ever so far away, as far as east from west, or heaven from earth, she would know him. To him she would be unchanged. The one beloved personality would stand out clear and firm amidst the chaos of delirious dreams. Much as he had prated of molecular action, and nerve messages, and all the machinery of materialism, he had expected here to find spirit working independently of matter, and love dominant over the laws of physiology.

The violet eyes, dilated by madness, looked at him, looked him through and through, and knew him not. She shrank from him with distrust, gathered up the scattered flowers in the

folds of her loose muslin gown, and moved hastily
from the table.

"I'm going to plant these in the front garden,
nurse," she said, "I want to get them planted
before father comes from the library. It'll be a
surprise for him, poor dear. He was grumbling
about the dust this morning, and saying how it
spoils everything, and he'll be pleased to see the
garden full of tulips and hyacinths. This sort
will grow without roots—they grow best without
roots, don't they?"

She looked down at the flowers dubiously, as
if not quite clear upon this point, and then with
a sudden vehemence ran to the fireplace, where
a small fire was burning behind a high brass
fender, and flung the tulips and hyacinths into
the fender.

"Oh, Mrs. Hanley, that's very naughty of you,"
cried the nurse, as if reproving a child, "to
throw away the pretty flowers that the Rector
brought you this morning. Why did you do
that, now?"

"I don't want them. They won't grow. It's
the day for my music lesson, and I haven't
practised. How cross Herr Schuter will be!"

There was a little cottage piano in a recess by the fireplace—a little old piano on which Miss Gilstone had practised her scales forty years before. Hester ran to the piano, seated herself hastily, and began to play one of Chopin's nocturnes—a piece so familiar in her girlhood that even in distraction some memory of the notes remained, and she played correctly and with feeling to the end of the first movement, when suddenly, at a loss for a bar, she burst into tears and left the piano.

"It is all gone," she said. "Why can't I remember?"

In all these varying moods and rapid movements about the room there had not been one look or one gesture which indicated consciousness of Gerard's presence. Those large, luminous eyes looked at him and saw him not, or saw him only as a stranger whose image awakened no interest.

The nurse dried the patient's tears and soothed her after that burst of grief at the piano, and a few minutes later Hester was standing at the open window tranquillised and smiling, watching for some one with an air of glad expectancy.

"How late he is," she said, "and I've got such a nice little dinner for him. I'm afraid it will be spoilt by waiting. It's the day the new magazines are given out at the Free Library. He is always late on magazine day. I ought to have remembered."

She turned quickly from the window and looked about the room.

"What has become of my sewing-machine?" she asked. "Have you taken it away?" to the nurse; "Or you?" to Gerard. "Pray bring it back directly, or I shall be behindhand with my work."

Her thoughts were all in the past, the days before she had entered into the tragedy of life, while yet existence was passionless, and meant only patience and duty. How strange it seemed to find her memory dwelling upon that dull time of drudgery and care, while the season of joy and love was forgotten.

"Is she often as restless as this?" he asked, with an agonised look at the doctor, who stood by the window, calmly watchful of his patient.

"Restless, do you call her? You would know what restlessness means if you had seen her three days ago, when the delirium was at its height, and one delusion followed another at lightning pace in that poor little head, and when it was all her two nurses could do to keep her from doing herself harm. She has improved wonderfully since then, and I am a great deal more hopeful about her."

"Have you had no second opinion? Surely in such a case as this a specialist should have been consulted?"

"We have had Dr. Campbell, the famous lunacy-doctor, whose opinion of the case corresponds with my own. There is very little to be done. Watchfulness and good nursing are all that we have to look to—and Nature, the great healer. I was right, you see. I told you she would not know you, and that seeing you could do her neither good nor harm."

"Yes, you were right. I am nothing to her —no more than if I had been a century dead— no more than any of the dead who are lying under those crumbling old tombstones yonder."

He glanced towards the churchyard, where the soft spring sunlight was shining upon grey granite and golden lichen, the dark foliage of

immemorial yews and the downy tufts upon the
young willows. He was standing side by side
with the woman who had loved him better
than her life, and she took no heed of him.
He tried to clasp her hand, but she moved
away from him, looking at him in shy surprise,
and with some touch of apprehension or dislike.

"Hester," he exclaimed piteously, "don't you
know me?"

"Are you another doctor?" she asked. "There
have been so many doctors—so many nurses—
and yet I am quite well. They have cut off
my hair, and they treat me as if I were a child
—but there is nothing the matter with me. I
don't want any more doctors."

"You see how she is," said Mr. Mivor. "I
think you had better come away at once. Your
presence excites her, although she doesn't know
you. Nothing can be done for her that is not
being done. Miss Gilstone has been all kindness. She has given up her sitting-room and
bedroom to your wife because they are the
prettiest in the house."

"She is an angel of charity," said Gerard,
"and Heaven knows how I can ever repay her."

"She is a Christian," said Mr. Mivor, "and she won't look to you for any reward. It is as natural for her to do good as it is for the flowers to bloom when their season comes."

Gerard followed the doctor out of the room, his looks lingering to the last upon the sweet pale face by the window, but the face gave no sign of returning memory. The doctor was right, no doubt. Messages of some kind were being carried swiftly enough along the nerve-fibres to the nerve corpuscles, but no message told of Gerard Hillersdon's existence, or of last year's love-story.

Gerard Hillersdon did not go back to London immediately after leaving the Rectory. He was fagged and faint after the long night of travel, the long morning of heart-rending emotions, the unaccustomed hurrying to and fro; but he had something to do that must be done, and with this business on his mind he had refused all offers of refreshment from the hospitable Rector, although he had eaten nothing since the hurried dinner in Paris on the previous night. He went from the Rectory at Lowcombe to the

Rose and Crown, in the next village, the inn
to which Hester had been carried after the
rescue from the river, and at which the inquest
upon her drowned baby had been held. He
went to that house thinking that there he would
be most likely to get the information he wanted
about the man who had saved Hester's life.

Life was saved, and reason might return; but,
alas, with returning reason would come the
mother's cry for the child her madness had
destroyed. Must she be told — or would she
remember what she had done? Would she
recall the circumstances of that fearful night,
and know that in her attempt to end her own
sorrows she had killed her innocent child?

To-day his business was to find out the name
of the man who had saved her life, possibly at
the hazard of his own; and he argued that the
Rose and Crown was the likeliest place at which
to get the information he wanted.

He was not mistaken. The inn was kept by
a buxom widow, who charged abnormal prices
for bedrooms in the boating season, and was
said to have fattened by picking the bones of
boating men. Although her bills were extor-

tionate her heart was beneficent, and she was eager to be serviceable to Mr. Hanley, of the Rosary. She expatiated tearfully upon the loveliness of the dear young lady who had been carried unconscious and apparently dead to the Rose and Crown's best bedroom. She dilated upon the efforts that had been made to bring life back to that cold form, and upon her own pious thankfulness when those efforts proved successful.

"Indeed, sir, I thought the dear young lady was gone," she said, "and if we hadn't had a medical student in the house who hurged us to go on"—the aspirate here seemed only an element of force—"and if we hadn't had the Newmane Serciety's instructions 'anging up in the 'all, I don't suppose we should ever have had the patience or the strength of mind to have kep' at it as we did."

"Can you tell me the name of the man who rescued her?" asked Gerard, somewhat curtly, considering the landlady's beneficence a matter to be settled like her bills, by a cheque.

"Why, of course I can, sir. He and his friend was obliged to stay the night in the 'ouse, for he'd nothing but his wet boating clothes and a overcoat. He stopped that night, and his clothes was dried at my own sitting-room fire, which I kep' up all night, on purpose, and he wrote his name in the visitors' book before he left next morning. I says, 'I should like to have your name in my book, sir, for you're a brave-hearted man.' And he laughs and says, 'Lor, landlady, you don't think what I've done anythink out of the way, do you? And as for my name,' he says, 'it's a very common one, but such as it is you're welcome to it."

The landlady produced a fat black quarto, in which amidst much sportive commendation of her meat and drink, and many fictitious entries of Dukes and Marquises, famous politicians, and notorious criminals, and a good deal of doggerel verse, there appeared the following modest entry—

Lawrence Brown, 49, Parchment Place, Inner Temple.

Gerard copied the address into his pocket-book, presented the mistress of the Rose and Crown with a bank note, for distribution among those servants who had been helpful on the night of the catastrophe, wished her good day, and was seated in his fly before she had time to steal a glance at the denomination of the note, or to give speech to her gratitude on discovering that it was not five, but five-and-twenty.

"This Mr. Hanley must be uncommonly rich to be so free with his money," she reflected, " but for all that I don't believe that pretty young creature is his wife. She wouldn't have took to wandering about with her baby if she had been. Perpetual fever says the doctor. Don't tell me ! Perpetual fever would never make a respectable married woman forget herself to that extent."

Two hours later Gerard Hillersdon was seated face to face with Lawrence Brown, barrister of no particular circuit, and of Parchment Place, Inner Temple.

The room was shabby almost to squalidness: the man was nearer forty than thirty, with roughly modelled features, keen eyes, intelligent brow, and dark hair already touched with grey about the temples.

He received Mr. Hillersdon's thanks politely, but with obvious reserve. He made very light of what he had done—no man seeing a life at stake could have done less. He was sorry—and here his face grew pale and stern—he had not been able to save the other life, the poor little child.

"My friend and I heard a child's faint cry," he said, "and it was that which called our attention to the spot, before we heard the splash. The current runs strong at that point. The woman rose, and sank again, twice before I caught hold of her, but the child was swept away upon the current. The body was found caught among the rushes half a mile lower down the stream."

There was a silence of some moments, during which Mr. Brown refilled his briarwood pipe, automatically, and looked at the little bit of fire burning dully in a rusty iron grate.

"Mr. Brown," began Gerard abruptly, "I am a very rich man."

"I am glad to hear it," replied Brown. "There are consolations in wealth which we poor men can hardly realise."

"You have called yourself a poor man," said Gerard, eagerly, "so you must not be angry with me if I presume to take that as a fact. I am rich, but my wealth is of very little use to me. I have had my death warrant. My time for spending money will soon be over, and my wealth must pass into other hands. I am here to beg your acceptance of a substantial reward for the act which has saved me from a burden that would have been unbearable—the thought that my absence from England had caused the death of the person who is dearer to me than any one else upon earth. Will you oblige me with your inkstand ? "

He stretched his hand towards a shabby china ink-pot in which half a dozen much-used quills kept guard over a thimbleful of ink.

" What are you going to do, Mr. Hanley ? "

" I am going to write a cheque, if you will allow me—a cheque for five thousand pounds, payable to your order."

" You are very good, but I am not a boatman, and I don't save lives for hire. I have not the faintest claim upon your purse. What I did for your—for Mrs. Hanley, I would have done for any love-sick kitchen-wench along the river. I heard a woman fall into the water, and I fetched her out. Do you suppose that I want to take money for that?"

"You would take a big fee for doing everything short of perjuring yourself in order to save the neck of a ruffianly burglar," said Gerard.

"I should do that in the way of business. It is my profession to defend burglars, and, short of perjury, to make believe that they are innocent and lamb-like."

"And you will not accept this recompense from me—a trifling recompense as compared with my income. You will not allow me to think that for once in a way my wealth has been of some service to a good man?"

"I thank you for your kind opinion of me, and for your wish to do me a kindness, but I cannot take a gift of money from you."

"Because you think badly of me?"

"I could not take a gift of money from any man who was not of my own blood, or so near and dear to me by friendship as to nullify all sense of obligation."

"But you could feel no obligation in this case, while your refusal to accept any substantial expression of my gratitude leaves me under the burden of a heavy obligation. Do you think that is generous on your part? "

" I am only certain of one thing, Mr. Hanley —I cannot accept any gift from you."

" Because you have a bad opinion of me. Come, Mr. Brown, between man and man, is not that your reason ? "

" You force me to plain speech," answered the barrister. " Yes, that is one of my reasons. I could not take a favour from a man I despise, and I can have no better feeling than contempt for the man who could abandon a friendless and highly strung girl in the day of trial—leave her to break her heart, and to try to make an end of herself in her despair."

" You are very ready with your summing up of my conduct. I was absent—granted; but I had left Mrs. Hanley surrounded with all proper care—— "

" You mean you had left her with a full purse and three or four servants. Do you think that means the care due from a husband to a wife who is about to become a mother ? You must not be surprised if I have formed my own opinion about

you, Mr. Hanley. I have been up and down the
river a good many times, and have lived for a
good many days here and there at riverside inns
within a few miles of the Rosary, and have heard
a good deal of talk about you and your lovely
wife—or not wife, as the case may be. The
village gossips would have it that she was not
your wife."

"The village gossips were right. I was bound
by an earlier claim, and I dared not marry her;
but if she and I live, and if I can release myself
from that other claim with honour, she shall be
my wife."

"I am glad to hear that. But I doubt if your
tardy reparation can ever efface the past."

The man was obviously so thoroughly in earnest
that even in the face of those shabby chambers,
that well-worn shooting-jacket and those much-
kneed trousers, Gerard could push his offer no
further. He might have been as rich as Roths-
child, and this man would have accepted not so
much as a single piece of gold out of his treasury.
There are men of strong feelings and prejudices
to whom money is not all in all; men who are
content to wear shabby tweed and trousers that

are bulging at the knees and frayed at the edge, and to sit beside a sparse fire in a rusty grate, and smoke coarse tobacco in an eighteen-penny pipe, so long as that inward fire of conscience burns bright and clear, and the silvering head can hold itself high in the face of mankind.

CHAPTER VII.

"THE LOVE THAT CAUGHT STRANGE LIGHT FROM DEATH'S OWN EYES."

GERARD HILLERSDON had no mind to occupy the cottage in which he had dreamed his brief love-dream, but he went to Lowcombe daily, and sat in the Rector's study, and heard the doctor's opinion, and the report of the nurses, and once on each day was admitted for a short time to the pretty sitting-room where Hester flitted from object to object with a feverish restlessness, or else sat statue-like by the open window gazing dreamily at churchyard or river.

The doctor and the nurses told him that there was a gradual improvement. The patient's nights were less wakeful, and she was able to take a little more nourishment. Altogether the case seemed hopeful, and even the violence of the earlier stages was said to predicate a rapid recovery.

"If she were always as you see her just now," said Mr. Mivor, glancing towards the motionless figure by the window, "I should consider her case almost hopeless—but that hyper-activity of brain which alarms you is an encouraging symptom."

The Rector was kind and sympathetic, but Gerard observed that Miss Gilstone avoided him. He was never shown into the drawing-room, but always into the Rector's study, where he felt himself shut out from social intercourse, as if he had been a leper. On his third visit he told the Rector that he was anxious to thank Miss Gilstone for her goodness to Hester; but the Rector shook his head dubiously.

"Better not think about it yet awhile," he said. "My sister is full of prejudices. She doesn't want to be thanked. She is very fond of this poor girl, and she thinks you have cruelly wronged her."

"People seem to have made up their minds about that," said Gerard. "I am not to have the benefit of the doubt."

"People have made up their minds that when a lovely and innocent girl makes the sacrifice that this poor girl has made for you, a man's conscience should constrain him to repair the wrong he has done—even though social circumstances make reparation a hard thing to do. But in this case difference of caste could have made no barrier. Your victim is a lady, and no man need desire more than that."

"There was a barrier," said Gerard. "I was bound by a promise to a woman who had been constant to me for years."

"But who had not sacrificed herself for you—as this poor girl has done. And it was because she was a clever, hard-headed woman of the world, perhaps, and had kept her name unstained, that you wanted to keep your promise to her, rather than that other promise—at least implied —which you gave to the girl who loved you."

Gerard was silent. What had he not promised in those impassioned hours when love was supreme? What pledges, what vows had he not given his fond victim, in that conflict between love and honour? She had been too generous ever to remind him of those passionate vows.

He had chosen to cheat her, and she had submitted to be cheated, resigned even to his abandonment of her if his happiness were to be found
elsewhere.

The London season had begun, and there were
plenty of people in town who knew Gerard Hillersdon, people who would have been delighted to
welcome him back to society after his prolonged
disappearance from a world which he—or at
any rate his breakfasts and dinners—had adorned.
But Gerard was careful to let no one know of his
return to London. The carriage gates of Hillersdon House were as closely shut as when the
master of the house was in Italy, and Mr. Hillersdon's only visitor entered by an insignificant
garden door which opened into a shabby street at
the back of the premises. This visitor was
Justin Jermyn, the confidant and companion
whose society was in some wise a necessity to
Gerard since his shattered nerves had made
solitude impossible. They dined together every
night, talked, smoked, and idled in a dreamy
silence, and played piquet for an hour or two
after midnight. The money he won at cards was

the only money that Jermyn had ever taken from his millionaire friend; but he was an exceptionally fine player, Gerard a careless one, and the stakes were high, whereby his winnings made a respectable revenue.

Gerard found Jermyn waiting for him when he returned, saddened and disheartened, from Lowcombe Rectory. Jermyn was sprawling on a sofa in the winter-garden, with his head deep in a leviathan pillow, and his legs in the air.

"There is a letter for you," he said, between two lazy puffs at a large cigar, "a letter from Florence — after Ovid, no doubt. Dido to Aeneas!"

"Why didn't you open it if you were curious?" sneered Gerard. "It would be no worse form than to pry into the address and postmark."

"There was no necessity; you are sure to tell me all about it."

The letter was from Mrs. Champion, and a thick letter, that lady scorning such small economy as the lessening of postage by the use of foreign paper.

"My Dear Gerard,

"I think my letter of last night may have prepared you in some degree for the letter I find myself constrained to write to-day. I might have hesitated longer, perhaps, had you been still at my side, might have trifled with your fate and mine, might have allowed myself to drift into a marriage which I am now assured could result in happiness neither for you nor me. The days are past in which you and I were all in all to each other. We are good friends still, shall be good friends, I hope, as long as we live; but why should friends marry, when they are happy in unfettered friendship?

"Your hurried departure makes my task easier; and should make the continuation of our friendship easier. When we meet again let us meet as friends, and forget that we have ever been more than friends. Day by day, and hour by hour, since you came to Florence it has been made clearer to my mind that we have both changed since last year. We are not to blame, Gerard, neither you nor I. The glamour has gone out of our lives somehow—we are 'the same and not the same.' I have seen coldness and·

despondency in you where all was once warmth and hope, and I confess that a coldness in my own heart responds to the chill that has come over yours. If we were to marry we should be miserable, and should perhaps come to hate each other before very long. If we are frank and straightforward, and true to each other at this crisis of our lives we need never be lessened in each other's esteem.

"I know that I have read your heart as truly as I have read my own; I do not, therefore, appeal to you for pardon. My release will be your release. Be as frank with me, my dear Gerard, as I have been with you, and send me a few friendly lines to assure me of kindly feeling towards your ever faithful friend,

"EDITH CHAMPION."

A deathlike chill crept through Gerard's veins as he read this letter to the end. The release as a release was welcome, but the underlying meaning of the letter, the feeling which had prompted it, cut him to the quick.

"She saw death in my face that first day at Florence," he told himself. "I could not mistake her look of horrified surprise, of repulsion almost, when I stood unexpectedly before her. She was able to hide her feelings afterwards, but in that moment love perished. She saw a change in me that changed her at once and for ever. I was not the Gerard Hillersdon of whom she had thought, and for whom she had waited. The man who stood before her was a stranger marked for death; a doomed wretch clinging to the hem of her garments to keep him from the grave—an embodied misery. Can I wonder that her heart changed to the man whom Death had changed?"

He read the letter a second time, slowly and thoughtfully. Yes, he could read between the lines. He had gone to his old love as an escape from death—a flight to sunnier skies, as the swallows fly to Africa. He had thought that somehow in that association with fresh and joyous life, he would escape out of the jaws of death, renew his boyish love, and with that renewal of youthful emotions renew youth itself. He had cheated himself with this hope when he turned his face towards Florence; but the woman he had loved, that bright embodiment of life and happiness, would have none of him.

Well, it was better so. He was free to pick
up the broken thread of that nearer, dearer, far
more enthralling love—if he could. If he could!
Can broken threads be united? He thought of
his child—his murdered child—murdered by his
abandonment of the mother. No act of his—no
tardy reparation—could bring back that lost life.
Even if Fate were kind, and Hester's health and
reason were restored, that loss was a loss for
ever, and would overshadow the mother's life to
the end.

He knew that he was dying, that for Hester
and him there could be no second summer of
happy unreasoning love. The meadow flowers
would blossom again ; the river would go
rippling past lawn and willowy bank under
the September sun ; but his feet would not
tread the ripe grasses, his voice would not
break the quiet of that lonely backwater where
Hester and he had dreamt their dream of a
world in which there was neither past nor future,
neither fear nor care, only ineffable love.

Jermyn watched him keenly as he walked up
and down the open space between a bank of vivid
tulips and a cluster of palms.

"Your letter seems to have troubled you," he said, at last. "Does she scold you for having run away just before your wedding? To-day was to have been the day, by the by."

"No, she is very kind—and very patient. She will wait till it suits me to go back."

"That will be next week, I suppose? You have done all you can do at Lowcombe. The *Jersey Lily* will suit you better than this house —delightful as it is—and Spezia or Sorrento will be a safer climate than London in May."

"I am in no hurry to go back—and I doubt if climate can make any difference to me."

"There you are wrong. The air a man breathes is of paramount importance."

"I will hear what my doctor says upon that point. In the meantime I can vegetate here."

He dined with Justin Jermyn. No one else knew that he was in London. He had not announced his return even to his sister, shrinking with a sense of pain from any meeting with that happy young matron, who was so full of the earnest realities of life, and who on their last meeting had asked such searching questions about her missing friend Hester, whether there was anything that she or her husband could do to find out the secret of her disappearance. She had reminded her brother that Jack Cumberland was the servant of Him who came to seek and to save those that were lost, and that even if Hester's footsteps had wandered from the right way, it was so much the more his duty to find her. Gerard had answered those eager questionings as best he might, or had left them unanswered; but he felt that in the present state of things he could scarcely endure to hear Hester's name, and that the mask must drop if he were called upon to talk about his victim.

Hester's attempted suicide, and the drowning of her child had not been made a local scandal, and bandied about in the newspapers. The fact was too unimportant to attract the attention of a metropolitan reporter, and Mr. Gilstone's wishes had been law to the editors of the two or three papers which usually concerned themselves with the affairs of Lowcombe and other villages within twenty miles of Reading. Gerard's domestic tragedy had therefore been unrecorded by the public Press.

The two young men went upstairs after dinner to smoke and lounge in the rooms which Gerard had copied from those unforgotten chambers in the old Inn. Here they usually sat of an evening, when they were alone; and it was here that most of those games of piquet had been played, the result of which had been to supply Justin Jermyn with a comfortable income without impoverishing the less successful player. But to-night Gerard was in no mood for piquet. His nerves were strained, and his brain was fevered. The game, which had generally a tranquillising influence, to-night only worried him. He threw his cards upon the table in a sudden fretfulness.

"It's no use," he said. "I hardly know what I am doing. I'll play no more."

He rose impatiently, and began to walk about the room, then stopped abruptly before a Japanese curtain, which hung against the panelling, and plucked it aside.

"Do you know what that is?" he asked, pointing to the sheet of drawing-paper scrawled with pen and ink lines.

"It looks as if it were meant for an outline

map. Your idea of Italy, perhaps, or Africa—drawn from memory, and not particularly like."

"It is my *peau de chagrin*—the talisman that shows the shrinking of vital force—vital force meaning life itself—and thus marks the swift passage to the grave. You see the outer line of all. Tolerably firm and free, is it not? Scarcely drawn by the hand of a Hercules, yet with no mark of actual feebleness. You see the inner lines, each following each, weaker and more irresolute, the last tremulous as a signature made on a death-bed."

He snatched a pen from the table near him, and dipped it in the ink, then made a dash at the chart, and tried to follow the outer line with a bolder sweep, but his arm was too weak to bear the strain of the upward position, and the pen ran down the paper with a single swift descending stroke, till it touched the outermost edge, then glanced off and dropped from the loosening hand.

"Do you see that?" he cried, with a burst of hysterical laughter. "The line goes down—straight as a falling star—as the life goes down to the grave."

"Come, come, my dear fellow, this is all womanish nonsense," said Jermyn, with his smooth somnolent voice, in whose sound there was a sense of comfort, as in the falling of summer rain. "You are tired. Lie down on this delightful sofa, and let me talk you to sleep."

He laid his hand on Gerard's shoulder with a friendly movement, and drew or led him to the capacious old Italian sofa, with its covering made of priestly vestments, still rich in delicate colouring, despite the sunlight and dust of centuries. Brain weary, and weak in body, Gerard sank on that luxurious couch, as Endymion on a bed of flowers, and the soft, slow music of Jermyn's voice—talking of the yacht, and the harbours where they two were to anchor along the shores of the Mediterranean—was potent as mandragora or moly. He sank into a delicious sleep—the first restful sleep he had known since he had left Florence.

It was ten o'clock when he fell asleep, and it was past eleven when he woke suddenly, his mind filled with one absorbing thought.

"My will!" he said; "I have made no will.

If I were to die suddenly—and with a weak heart who can tell when death may come—I should die intestate. That would be horrible. I have settled something—but not much; not enough"—this to himself, rather than to Jermyn, who sat quietly beside the sofa, watching him, "I must make a will."

No such thought had been in his mind before he fell asleep; no idea of any such necessity. If he had thought—as a millionaire must think —of the disposal of his money, he had told himself that were he to die intestate his father would inherit everything, and that having provided for Hester's future by a deed of trust, it mattered little whether he made a will or not. A few casual friends would be cheated of expected legacies—but that mattered little. He had no friends—not even this umbra of his, Justin Jermyn—whose disappointment mattered to him. But to-night his whole mind was absorbed in the necessity of disposing of his fortune. He was fevered with impatience to get the thing done.

"Give me a sheet of that large paper," he said, pointing to his writing-table. "I will make my will at once. You and a servant can witness it. A holograph will is as good as any, and there is no one who could attack my will."

"I hope you won't ask me to witness the document," said Jermyn, laying a quire of large Bath Post before Gerard, with inkstand and blotter, "for that would mean that you are not going to leave me so much as a curio or a mourning ring."

"True—I must leave you something. I'll leave you your own likeness—the faun yonder," said Gerard, looking up at the bust, the laughing lips in marble seeming to repeat Jermyn's broad smile.

"You must leave me something better than that. I am as poor as Job, and if I outlive you where will be my winnings at piquet? Leave me the scrapings of your money bags. Make me residuary legatee, after you have disposed of your fortune. The phrase will mean very little, though it sounds big—but there must be some scrapings."

Gerard opened an enamelled casket, a master work of the cinque-cento goldsmiths, and took out a long slip of paper, the schedule of his possessions, a catalogue of stocks and shares, in his own neat penmanship. A glance along this row of figures showed him where his wealth lay, and with this slip of paper spread on the table before him he began to write.

To my father, the Reverend Edward Hillersdon, Rector of Helmsleigh, in Consols, so much, in South-Western Ordinary Stock—in Great Western—Great Eastern—Great Northern, so much, and so much, and so much, till he had disposed of the first million, Justin Jermyn standing by his side and looking down at him, with his hand on his shoulder.

He no longer wrote the small neat hand which had once penned a popular love-story, and almost made its owner a name in literature. To-night, in his fever and hurry of brain, his writing sprawled large over the page—the first page was covered with the mere preliminary statement of sound mind, etc., etc., and his father's name. Then came the list of securities, covering three other pages—then to my sister Lilian, wife of John Cumberland, vicar of St. Lawrence, Soho, and then another list of securities—then to my mother, all my furniture, pictures, plate, in my

house at Knightsbridge, with the exception of
the marble faun in my study—then to my beloved
friend, Hester Davenport, fifty thousand pounds
in Consols, and my house and grounds at Lowcombe, with all contents thereof—and, finally,
to Justin Jermyn, whom I appoint residuary
legatee, the marble faun. One after another, as
the pages were finished in the large hurried
penmanship, Justin Jermyn picked them up, and
dried them at the wood fire. The nights were
chilly, though May had begun, and Gerard's sofa
had been drawn near the hearth.

It was on the stroke of midnight when the will
was ready for signature.

"Kindly ring, Jermyn. My valet will be up,
of course, and most of the other servants, perhaps,
for this is a dissipated house. I hear them
creeping up to bed at midnight very often when
I am sitting quietly here. The servants' staircase is at this end of the house."

"Talking of staircases, you haven't left Larose
so much as a curio," said Jermyn, as he pressed
a bronze knob beside the mantelpiece.

"Why should I leave him anything? He has
made plenty of money out of this house. Do

you think I want to give him a pleasant half-hour, when I am in my grave?"

"I thought you liked him."

"I like no one, in the face of death," answered Gerard, fiercely. "Do you think I can love the men whose lives are long—who are to go on living and enjoying for the greater part of a century, perhaps, to be recorded approvingly in the *Times* obituary, after drinking the wine of life for ninety years, 'We regret to announce the death of Archdeacon So-and-so, in his eighty-ninth year'? Regrets for a man of eighty-nine! And you think that I, who am doomed to die before I am thirty, can feel kindly towards the long-lived of my species! Why should one man have so much, and I so little?"

"Why should one man be an agricultural labourer with fifteen shillings a week for his highest wage, while you have two millions?"

"Money! Money is nothing! Life is the only thing that is precious. Death is the only thing that is horrible."

"True; and I doubt if the man of ninety is any more in love with death than you are at nine-and-twenty."

" Oh, but he is worn out; he must know that. The machine has done its work, and perishes of fair wear and tear. It doesn't go to pieces suddenly because of a flaw in the metal. I grant that it is a hideous thought that life should end —ever; that this Ego, so strong, so distinct, so vivid and all-absorbing, should go out with a snap into unknown darkness; but to die young, to die before wrinkles and grey hairs, to die while life is still fresh and beautiful—that is hard. I almost hate my own father when I think by how many golden years he may survive me, and revel in this wealth that was mine. They will make him a bishop, perhaps. Who knows? A rich man must always be a power in the Church. My father would make an admirable bishop. He will live as long as Martin Routh, I dare say—live on into the new century, opulent, portly, benevolent, happy—while I am nothing! Oh, think how hard these differences are! Think of Shelley's heart turned to dust under the stone in the Roman graveyard, and Shelley's friend living for sixty years after him, to lie down tired and full of years beside him who went out in water and flame, like the bright wild spirit he was."

Jermyn laid his hand upon him soothingly, yet with something of imperiousness. "Be calm," he said; "you have to sign these sheets."

The door opened, and the valet whose duty it was to answer his master's bell in the late evening came quietly into the room.

"Are there any of the servants still up?" asked Jermyn.

"Burton has not gone to bed yet, sir.",

"Then ask Burton to come here with you to witness some papers. He is sober enough to remember what he does, I suppose?"

"Sober, sir? Yes, sir; I never saw Burton otherwise," replied the valet, with dignity.

"Be quick, then," said Jermyn. "Your master is waiting."

His master waited very patiently, with fixed and dreamy eyes, his hand lying loose upon the first sheet of the will, as Jermyn had placed it before him. Jermyn stood at his elbow, holding the other leaves of the will in his left hand, while his right rested lightly upon Gerard's shoulder.

The valet returned, accompanied by the butler,

who looked solemn, and was careful to abstain from speech.

He stood at attention, breathing brandy, but the penmanship with which he witnessed his master's signature, as the sheets were signed one after another, was not illegible.

The valet signed with a steady hand and a bold front. He, too, had been drinking heavily, but he had a more delicate taste in liquors than his fellow-servant.

"You may as well understand the nature of this document," said Jermyn to the witnesses, " but it is not legally necessary that you should do so. It is your master's will. The only will you have made, I think, Hillersdon," he added, with his hand still lying upon Gerard's shoulder, a large hand, with abnormal length of finger, and deadly white.

" It is the only will I have made," Gerard said slowly.

" Or intend to make."

" Or intend to make," replied Gerard.

" You can go,"' said Jermyn to the men, "I am to sleep here to-night, by the way."

"Yes, sir. Your room is ready. I have put out your things."

Jermyn had been staying in the house since his return from Italy, but in a casual way, and he had daily talked of going to his own chambers. He had rooms somewhere in the neighbourhood of Piccadilly, but rarely imparted the secret of his address, and had never been known to entertain anybody except at a club. Gerard's single experience of his hospitality had been that after-midnight supper in the chambers eastward of Lincoln's Inn.

" You are very tired, my dear fellow," said Jermyn, when the servants were gone.   " You had better lie down again."

Gerard rose out of his chair, leaving the loose sheets of Bath Post lying on the table, without so much as a look at them, and Jermyn slipped an arm through his and led him back to the sofa, where he sank down with closing eyelids, and was deep asleep a few moments later.

Jermyn took up the loose pages, folded them carefully, put them in an inner pocket of his dinner jacket, and went out of the room. The valet was waiting on the landing.

" Your master has fallen asleep on the sofa," said Jermyn.   " He seems very much exhausted,

and I think you had better let him stay there all
night rather than disturb him. You can put a
rug over him, and leave him till the morning.
He is not ill, only tired. I'll look in upon him
now and then in the night. I'm a very light
sleeper."

The valet paused, anxious to get to bed, yet
doubtful.

"Do you really think he will require nothing,
sir?"

"Nothing but sleep. He is thoroughly worn
out. A long night's rest will do wonders for
him."

The valet submitted to a friendly authority.
Mr. Jermyn wore his hair very short, had a
scientific air, and was doubtless half a doctor.
The valet went to look at his master, and
covered him carefully with a soft Indian rug.
Certainly that deep and peaceful sleep was not
to be rudely broken. It was a sleep that might
mean healing.

It was ten o'clock next morning before Gerard
awoke. Mr. Jermyn had gone into the study
several times during the night, but at ten he
left the house, and it was only as the outer door

closed upon him that Gerard began to stir in his sleep, and presently opened his eyes and got up, wondering to see the morning sunlight stealing through the Venetian shutters, and making golden bars upon the sombre carpet.

He looked at the clock. Ten, and broad daylight. He had slept nine hours, yet with no consciousness of more than the light and brief slumber of a man who throws himself upon his sofa for a casual nap. A sleep without dreams— a mere gap in life—that blank and idealess slumber which Socrates declared to be the equivalent of supremest earthly bliss.

"I never slept so many hours on end in my life," he said to himself, almost appalled at his abnormal slumber.

He looked about the room, slowly recalling the events of yesterday. His journey to Lowcombe, his return to town, the letter from Edith Champion.

He felt in his pocket for the letter. Yes, it was there. He read it a third time hurriedly. He wanted to be sure that he was a free man.

"Free as air," he told himself, "whistled down the wind to prey at fortune. Free to marry the woman 1 love—free to set right her wrongs."

To right her wrongs! Could he bring his drowned child back to life—could he heal the mother's shattered brain? Such wrongs can never be righted. The scar they leave is deadly.

He thought over the words of Edith's letter, so cold in their hard, common sense; and then he recalled his own image as he had seen it in the glass that first afternoon in the Florentine villa. That face of his, with death written upon it, was enough to scare away love. He was contemptuous and angry as he thought of that summer-time love; so exacting, so jealous, so insistent, while the sun of life and youth rode high in the cloudless heaven; so quick to faint and fail when the shadows fell.

Of the will made at midnight he had not a moment's thought. Upon that point memory was a blank. Nor did he make any inquiry about Jermyn. He dressed, breakfasted, and was on the way to Lowcombe before noon.

There was no change in the patient, but the doctor was not unhopeful. Progress must needs be slow, and it was well if there were no retrograde steps.

" Time is now the only healer we can look to," said Mr. Mivor.

There was a considerable change in the Rector after half an hour's confidential talk with Gerard; and Miss Gilstone, who hitherto had kept herself out of Mr. Hillersdon's way, received him in her drawing-room, and talked with him for more than an hour, graciously accepting his thanks for all her goodness to Hester.

"Be assured I would have done as much for the poorest girl in the parish, if her sorrows had appealed to me as Hester's did," said Miss Gilstone, " but I don't mind confessing that her beauty and her sweetness have made a profound impression upon me. Poor soul, even in her worst hours every word she spoke helped to show us the gentleness and purity of her nature. I could but think of what Ophelia's brother said of his sister,

> ' Thought and affliction, passion, hell itself,
> She turns to favour, and to prettiness.'

Oh, Mr. Hanley, it would be an awful thought for you in after years to have led such a girl

astray, and not to have made the utmost reparation in your power."

"It would have been—it is an awful thought,"
Gerard answered dejectedly. "My only desire
now is that I may live long enough to make
Hester my wife. The day she first recognises
me, the day she is in her right mind, I am ready
to marry her. The Rector has asked me to be
his guest, so that I may know how she progresses
hour by hour. Shall I be in your way, Miss
Gilstone, if I venture to accept his invitation?"

"In my way? No indeed. As if any one my
brother likes to ask could ever be in my way.
Why, he and I have never had two opinions
about anything or anybody in our lives. We
are not like the husbands and wives, who seldom
seem to think alike."

"Then I may stay."

"Of course you may. Your room is being got
ready; and we can put up your servant if you
like to bring him."

"You are too good; but I have no need of a
servant. I shall not impose upon your kindness
further than by my own presence."

He sauntered in the churchyard with the

Rector during the balmy hour before sunset, and
in that hour he told Mr. Gilstone his name and
his history, frankly and fully, holding back
nothing of folly or selfishness, greed of pleasure
or greed of wealth.

"Do not think too meanly of me if I confess
to having envied my rich friends their wealth, at
the University and in the world. The greed of
gold is the vice of the age we live in. The air is
charged with bullion. All life is flavoured with
the follies and extravagances of the newly rich.
Everything is given and forgiven to the millionaire. For one Nero, with his Golden House,
we have Neros by the score, and whole streets of
golden houses. For one Lucullus we have an
army of dinner-givers, at whose tables the para-
site fattens. It is not possible for a young man
to live in the stress and turmoil of London
society and not hanker after gold as the one
supreme good, and not ache with the pangs of
poverty. The time came when I meant to blow
my brains out, because it was better to be dead
and dust than alive and poor. And on that day
of despair Fortune turned her wheel, and be-
behold! I was a double millionaire. But

scarcely had I tasted the rapture of wealth before I was told that my life was not worth two years' purchase ; and from that hour to this I have lived with one dark spectre always at my elbow."

"I have seen so many peaceful death-beds that I can hardly realise the fear of death," said the Rector, "any more than I can conceive the fear of sleep."

"Ah, but the everlasting sleep, that's the rub. Not the dreams that Hamlet talks about, but the dreamless blank ! 'This sensible warm motion to become a kneaded clod !' To give up everything ! "

"Hard indeed, if we had no hope of fairer worlds."

"A hope ! A mirage, Mr. Gilstone. I can fully understand that it is your duty, as a minister of the Gospel, to hold that mirage before the dying eyes of your parishioners. But do you mean to tell me, after your long life of knowledge and of thought, that the fantastic vision of an after-world can be any comfort to you ? Where is the link that can unite the dwindling dust below those grave-stones with other planets or with future time? New worlds and fairer there may be; new stars may teem with beings of grander frame and nobler minds than ours, star after star, in endless evolution, till there be worlds peopled with gods; but for me, for you, for this dust here, there is nothing more. We have no more account in those glories to come than last summer's butterflies have. We have had our day. Do you remember how Cæsar urged that Cataline and his followers should be punished in their lives, not by death, since death is only the release from suffering, and beyond death there is no place either of joy or sorrow? And you think because ninety years after Cæsar spoke those words a village carpenter, gifted beyond the average of highly gifted humanity, codified the purest system of morals ever revealed to man, and threw out random hints of a future existence, and because in after-generations tradition ascribed to this gifted man a miraculous return from death to life—you think, because Jesus talked of a day of judgment and an after-world, that the stern truths of science and fact are to weigh as nothing against those vague promises of a rustic teacher?"

"My dear friend, I will not admit that science

has all the strongest arguments on her side, and that faith can only sit with folded hands and wait—

> ' The Shadow, cloak'd from head to foot,
> Who keeps the keys of all the creeds ; '

but I am no dialectician, and will not attempt to argue against the barren creed which modern metaphysicians give out with as much delight as if they were bringing us new hopes instead of trying to kill the old ones. I will only say, as St. Paul said, 'If in this life only we have hope in Christ we are of all men most miserable.' ”

“ St. Paul was a dreamer and an enthusiast ; just the right man to make a new religion ; an intellectual force, great enough to change the face of Europe, and last nineteen hundred years. But I fear the axe is laid to the root of the tree, and that before the twentieth century is sped Christianity will be at best a State religion— a system of ceremonials and embroidered vestments, as it was in Pagan, as it is in Papal Rome.”

The tranquil monotony of life at Lowcombe Rectory was not unpleasing to Gerard. His health was too weak for London pleasures. It suited him best to spend his days in a dreamy idleness, nursing his shrunken stock of vitality as the poor sempstress nurses her tiny fire, lest the pitiful half hundred of coal should burn too quickly. He was glad to be away from the gay world, and from the house whose splendours and luxuries had long palled upon him. Here, at least, he had rest. Even the rustic simplicity of his surroundings had a soothing influence, recalling his childish days in the old parsonage beside the mouth of the Exe. Here he was at peace, and here he was able to face the inevitable with more resignation than he had felt hitherto.

He knew that he had not long to live. He had seen Dr. South once again since his return to England, and had heard the verdict which he meant to be final. He would question science no more, since science could do so little for him, giving him at most certain rules of dietary, and a prescription which any village druggist could make up. He had to face a future which might be but a few weeks, or which, if he were careful, and Fate and climate were kind, might be spun out yet a little longer.

Here, sauntering by the river on the bright May mornings, he was able to plan that remnant of life, as it was to be spent when Hester should be restored to health and reason, and might go with him where he pleased. He would not lose an hour in making her his lawful wife, and then he would take her to Spezia as fast as boat and train could carry them, and instal her in the luxurious nest which had been prepared for another bride. And then they two would sail away together to the fairest shores of the fair inland sea, and so, death kept at bay to the utmost, should at last come upon him with gentlest aspect, and find him in his wife's fond arms, her tender hand wiping the last dews from his brow, her kisses on his darkening eyelids.

He revisited some of the old spots where he had walked with Hester in the late summer time of last year, and these rambles gave him only too just a measure of his vanishing strength. The fields over which he had trodden so lightly last September seemed now an impossible journey. He was fain to haunt the willowy bank between the churchyard and the Rosary, a distance of less than a mile. This marked the limit of his power, and he had often to rest in the Rosary garden before he could attempt the walk back to the Rectory.

The garden was in perfect order, as in the days when Hester had moved about it, "Queen rose of the roses." Everything was to be kept as it had been under her brief tenancy of the house that he had bought for her. She might wish to go back there some day, despite all that she had suffered within those walls. In any case it was her home, and he desired that it should be kept in order for her. In all this time he had ignored his own kindred. His mother and father, Lilian and her husband knew nothing of his return to England. He meant to see his sister again, were it only for half an hour, before he went back to Italy; but he did not want to see her until Hester was his wife, and he could bring sister and wife together. He wanted to secure this one faithful friend for Hester before he died.

At last, after a long month of hope and expectancy the happy chance came. Hester's wearied brain slowly awakened from its troubled sleep, and memory and recognition of familiar faces came back one summer morning with the opening of the June roses that clustered about her window.

"Gerard," she cried, looking up at him affectionately, as he stood beside her chair, where he had so often waited for the faintest sign of returning memory. "You have come back from Italy at last! How long you have been away. How dreadfully long!"

He sat with her for an hour talking of indifferent things. Memory came back gradually. It was not till the next day that she remembered her father's death, and the doctor hoped that the night of her wandering by the river, and the loss of her baby, would be blotted out. But that was not to be. As her mind recovered its balance the memory of all she had suffered and done in the long hours of delirium came back with agonising distinctness. She remembered the watchful care of her nurses, which had seemed to her a cruel tyranny. She remembered creeping out of the house, and through the darkness of the dewy garden, and along by the river, to that favourite spot where she and Gerard had spent so many happy hours. She remembered how she had thought that death was best for her and for her

child, the one refuge from a world in which no
one loved them or wanted them, she a deserted
mistress, he a nameless child.   She remembered
the plunge in the darkness, the buoyant feeling
of the water as it wrapped her round—and then
no more, except the monotony of quiet days and
kindly faces, sunlit rooms and sweet-scented
flowers at the Rectory, a time in which she had
for the most part fancied herself a child again,
sinless, happy, full of childish thoughts.

They were married in the shadowy old parish
church at half-past eight o'clock one June morning, Hester, pale and wan, but with a delicate
loveliness which ill-health could not spoil.   She
was dressed in a grey tweed gown, and neat little
hat, ready for a long journey.   Gerard was flushed
and anxious-looking, hollow-eyed and hollow-
cheeked, and far more nervous than his wife.

They drove from the church to the station on
their way to London, charged with many bless-
ings from the Rector and his sister, who, with
the parish clerk, had alone witnessed the
ceremony.

" She is fast your wife," quoted the Rector,

"the finest choral service in Westminster Abbey could not make the bond any stronger."

Gerard had telegraphed to his sister to meet him at luncheon at Hillersdon House, where he and Hester arrived between twelve and one.

He spent the hour before Lilian's arrival in showing Hester his house.

"It is yours now," he said, "yours as much as the Rosary, which I bought to be your plaything. It will be yours for many a year, 1 hope, when I am at rest."

She gave him a heart-rending look. Could he think that this splendour would comfort her when he was gone—or that she could ever cease to think of him and of her child—the child her madness had sacrificed? She would not pain him by one mournful word, on this day above all other days, when he had done all that he could do to give her back her good name. She went with him from room to room, praising his taste, admiring this and that, till she came to his sanctum on the upper floor.

She had scarcely crossed the threshold when she saw the faun, and gave a little cry of disgust.

"Mr. Jermyn," she said.

"Only a chance likeness—but a good one, ain't it?"

"Why do you have his likeness in your room? It is an odious face, and he is a hateful man. I cannot understand how you could ever have chosen him for your friend."

"He has never been my friend, Hester. I have no friend but Mr. Gilstone. That old man is the first person from whom I have experienced real friendliness since I became a millionaire. Jermyn has been my companion—an amusing companion—and I have never found any harm in him."

Hester looked at everything with fond interest. It was here he had lived before he knew her. It was this luxurious nest he had left for his riverside home with her. She looked at the books, and the curios on the carved oak cabinet, bronzes, ivories, jade; and finally stopped before a curtain of Japanese embroidery, which hung against the panelling.

"Is there a picture behind this curtain," she asked, "a picture which no one must look at without permission?"

"No, it is not a picture. You may look if you

like, Hester. I have no secrets from the other half of my soul."

Hester drew back the curtain, and saw a large sheet of drawing paper, scrawled over with black lines, conspicuous among them a long downward sweep of the pen, thick and blurred.

"What a curious thing," she cried. "What does it mean?"

"It is the chart of my life, Hester. The downward stroke means the end."

He ripped the sheet off the panel upon which it had been neatly fastened with tiny copper nails, and then tore it into fragments and flung them into the waste-paper basket.

"I am reconciled to the end, Hester," he said softly, as she clung to him, hiding her tears upon his shoulder, "now that you and I are together —will be together to the last."

He heard Lilian's step upon the stair, and in another minute she was in the room, looking at Hester in glad astonishment.

"Hester! He has found you then, and all is well," cried Lilian, "but, oh, my poor dear, how pale and wan you are looking. Has the world gone so badly with you since we met?"

"Ask her no questions, Lilian, but take her to your heart as your sister and my wife."

"Your wife—since when, Gerard?"

"That is a needless question. She is my wife —my loved and honoured wife."

Lilian looked at him wonderingly for a moment. Yes, he was in earnest evidently, and this union of which she had never dreamed was an actuality. She turned to Hester without a word and kissed her.

"You shall be to me as a sister," she said gently, "and I will not ask you what trouble has made you so sad and pale, or why my brother has kept his marriage a secret from me until to-day."

After this they went downstairs to luncheon, a luncheon at which but little was eaten, yet which was the happiest meal Gerard had shared in for many a day. That shadow of the past which darkened Hester's life touched him but lightly. For him the future was so brief that the past mattered very little. He could not feel any poignant regret for the child whose face he had never seen; for had that child lived his part in the young fresh life would have been too brief to reckon. The son could have never known a father's love.

They left for Turin by the evening train, Lilian only parting with them at the station, where the two pale faces vanished from her view, side by side. One of those faces she had faintest hope of ever seeing again in this world.

EPILOGUE.

THE London season was waning, and Justin Jermyn was beginning to talk about taking his cure—of nothing particular—in the Pyrenees, when the gossips of those favourite literary, artistic, and social clubs, the Sensorium and the Heptachord, were interested by a brief announcement in the *Times* list of deaths.

"On July 19th, on board the *Jersey Lily*, at Corfu, Gerard Hillersdon, aged 29."

"So that is the end of Hillersdon's luck," said Larose, "and one of the most live-able houses in London will come into the market. It is only a year and a half since it was finished, and we spent his money like water, I can assure you. We could hardly spend it fast enough to please him. The sensation was delicious from its novelty."

" What was his luck ? Got a million or so left him for picking up an old chap's umbrella, wasn't it ? "

" No ; he saved the old man's life, and almost missed the fortune by *not* picking up the umbrella."

" Mr. Jermyn loses a useful friend. He was always about with Hillersdon. And who gets all the money ? Or did Hillersdon contrive to run through it ? "

" Not he," said a gentleman of turfy tastes. " He was a poor creature, and I don't believe he ever backed a horse from the day he left Oxford. Such a man couldn't spend a million, much less two millions. He was the sort of fellow who would economise and live upon the interest of his money. Those are not the men who make history."

" He began his career as a scribbler," said some one else. " Wrote a sentimental story, and set all the women talking about him, and then took to writing for the papers, and was in very low water when he came into his millions."

"He ought to have run a theatre," said another.

"Not he! The man didn't know how to spend money. He was distinguished in nothing."

"He gave most delightful breakfasts," said Larose.

"Yes, to half a dozen fellows who talk fine, like you and Reuben Gambier. I say he was a poor creature, upon whom good luck was wasted."

This was the final verdict of the smoking-room. The dead man had wasted golden opportunities.

It was on the same day that Mr. Crafton, of Messrs. Crafton and Cranberry, Lincoln's Inn Fields, received a visitor, who called by appointment, made by telegraph that morning. The visitor was Justin Jermyn, whom Mr. Crafton had met only once in his life at a dinner given by his client, Gerard Hillersdon.

The solicitor received Mr. Jermyn with grave cordiality, the recent death of an important client demanding an air of suppressed mournfulness.

"Sad news from Corfu," said Jermyn. "You saw the announcement in the *Times*, of course?"

"Yes; but it was not news to me. I had a telegram within two hours of the event—which was not unexpected. Our client has been slowly fading out of life ever since he left England in June. You have not been yachting with him, Mr. Jermyn?" interrogatively.

"No; I have written to him two or three times offering myself for a short cruise. It was I who bought the yacht for him, and superintended her fitting out. But his replies were brief, and"—with something of his familiar laugh, subdued to meet the circumstances—"he evidently didn't want me; but as there was a lady in the case I was not offended. Well, he is gone, poor fellow. A brilliant life, only too brief. One would rather jog on for a dull fourscore, even without his supreme advantages."

There was a pause. Mr. Crafton looked politely anticipative of he knew not what. And then, as the other sat smiling and did not speak, he himself began—

"You may naturally suppose, that, as a friend of Mr. Hillersdon's, you may have been remembered for some graceful gift, or even a money legacy," he said blandly, " but I am sorry to tell you there are no such gifts or legacies. Our lamented client died intestate."

" How do you know that—and so soon ? " asked Jermyn, still smiling.

" We have the fact under his own hand, in a letter dated only three days before his death. The letter is here," taking it from a brass rack on the table. " I will read you the passage."

He cleared his throat, sighed, and read as follows—

" ' My doctor, who has been hinting at wills and testaments for the last month, tells me that if I have to make my will I must make it without loss of an hour. But I am not going to make any will. My fortune will go just where I am content that it shall go, and I can trust those who will inherit to deal generously with others whom I might have named had I nerved myself to the horror of will-making. I would as soon assist in the making of my coffin. I shall leave it to my father to make a suitable acknowledg- ment, on my behalf, to you and Mr. Cranberry, whose disinterested care of my estate,' hum, hum,

hum," murmured the lawyer, folding the letter. "I need read no further."

"No. It is a curious thing that a man should write those words who had three months before made a holograph will, and had it duly witnessed, in my presence."

"When was this?"

"On the third of May in this year."

"You surprise me. Were you one of the witnesses?"

"Certainly not."

"And how did you know of the will?"

"I was present when it was made, and it was given into my possession. I have brought it to you, Mr. Crafton, in order that you may do as much for me as you did two years ago for my lamented friend, Gerard Hillersdon."

He handed the lawyer a document which consisted of only two sheets of Bath Post, each sheet in Gerard Hillersdon's handwriting, and each sheet duly signed and attested.

The first sheet set forth the nature of the testator's possessions, a list of securities; the second sheet bequeathed these to "Justin Jermyn, of 4, Norland Court, Piccadilly, whom I appoint my residuary legatee."

"That will is good enough to stand, I think, Mr. Crafton."

"An excellent will, although he does not particularise half his property."

"No; but I think the words residuary legatee will cover everything."

"Assuredly. Was he of sound mind when he made this will?"

"He was never of unsound mind within my knowledge. You had better question the witnesses, his valet and his butler, as to his mental condition on the evening of May the third."

"I will not trouble them. I am sorry for your disappointment, Mr. Jermyn, though less sorry than I might have been had you a nearer claim on our deceased client. This will is waste paper."

"The devil it is? You don't pretend there is any subsequent will?"

"Not unless one was made after the letter I have read to you. Your will is rendered invalid by our client's marriage."

"His marriage?"

"Yes. He was married on the third of June, at the Parish Church of Lowcombe, Berkshire.

He kept his marriage dark, I know. There was no announcement in the papers. The lady was in poorish circumstances, I fancy, and the marriage altogether a romantic affair. She has been with him on his yacht ever since."

"With him. Yes, I knew that she was with him. But his wife! That's a fiction."

"If it is, one of the most genuine-looking marriage certificates I ever handled is a forgery. I have the certificate in my possession, sent to me by the clergyman who performed the ceremony. Mr. Hillersdon having died intestate, his fortune, real and personal—there was very little real property by the way—will be divided between his father and his wife. Your only chance now, Mr. Jermyn, would be to try and marry the widow."

"Thanks for the advice. No, I don't think I should have much chance there. Well, I have lost friend and fortune—but I am here, and life is sweet. I am not dashed by your news, Mr. Crafton, though it is somewhat startling. Good day."

He laughed his gnomish laugh, took up his hat in one hand and waved the other to the lawyer, with the lightest gesture of adieu, and so vanished, joyous and tranquil to the last—a man without conscience and without passion.

And what of Hester, enriched beyond the dreams of womanly avarice, but widowed in the morning of her life? Can there be happiness for that lonely heart, charged with sad memories?

Yes, there is at least the happiness of a life devoted to good works, a life divided between the rural quiet of the village by the Thames and those crowded alleys and shabby slums in which John Cumberland and his young wife labour, and in which Hester is their devoted and zealous lieutenant. In every scheme for the welfare of innocent little children, in every effort for the rescue of erring women and girls, Hester is an intelligent and unwearying helper. She does not scatter her wealth blindly or weakly. She is not caught by flowery language or flatteries addressed to her feminine vanity. She brings brain as well as heart to bear upon the business of philanthropy, and in all her dealings with the poor she has the gift of insight, which is second only to her gift of sympathy.

If to help others in their sorrow is to be happy, Hester should attain happiness; but there are those who see upon the fair young face the sign and token of early death; and in those meadow paths, and by the river where she and Gerard walked in their summer dream of a deathless love it may be that those pathetic eyes of hers already see the shadow of the end.

She brought her husband from the lovely land where he died to lay him in Lowcombe Church-yard, and the summer sun seldom goes down without glorifying one quiet figure, seated or kneeling in the secluded shelter of a great yew tree, by Gerard Hillersdon's grave.

THE END.

LONDON: PRINTED BY WILLIAM CLOWES AND SONS, LIMITED,
STAMFORD STREET AND CHARING CROSS.

www.ingramcontent.com/pod-product-compliance
Lightning Source LLC
Chambersburg PA
CBHW020105030726
47498CB00006B/1953